BOOK OF CERBERUS

ATTICUS BLACKWOOD

CONTENTS

Chapter 1
Last Day of School

I was restlessly gazing at the clock, willing time to pass more quickly, but it seemed as if Kronos himself was purposefully stretching out the minutes to torment me. While contemplating whether to retrieve my copy of "The Hero with a Thousand Faces" by Joseph Campbell, I glanced around the room. My classmates were all lost in their own activities, eagerly anticipating the end of the school day since it was the last day before the summer break; it was also a half day, so we would get out around 12 pm.

Some of the boys were engrossed in a card game in the corner of the classroom, while most of the girls were busy fixing their makeup in small handheld mirrors. The extent to which they focused on their appearance puzzled me, given that we were only ninth graders with no elaborate social events on the horizon. For me, makeup was never a priority, especially given the limited availability of shades suitable for my dark skin tone. Besides, there was no one special to impress.

My train of thought then turned to the upcoming weekend, realizing that I needed to find time to get my hair braided to manage the persistent tangle of curls that had been bothering me all semester. As

I shifted my attention, I wondered about Mr. Barnes, our history teacher. Considering his penchant for summer travels, I found myself contemplating what exciting adventures he and his wife might embark on. However, the evidence of his aging appearance made me wonder if their plans might be more subdued. Despite his advancing years, I mused that a change of scenery and a touch of sun could do him good.

Reflecting on the classes at Pine Ridge High School, I couldn't help but concede my hatred to most of them. However, Mr. Barnes' class was an exception. His incorporation of mythology into his teaching style always captivated me, as I had a deep passion for ancient myths and legends. The old tales of heroes and monsters fired my imagination, and some days, I found myself yearning for those myths to come to life. In a world where the monsters were just school bullies and the protective armor was nothing more than our school uniform, the dull white collared shirts, red and yellow striped ties, and gray skirts and trousers felt like symbols of the conformity the school system enforced.

Suddenly, a loud bell through the hallway, signaling the end of the school day. In a frenzy, students hastily snatched their bags and sprinted out through the doorway. Just as I was about to join the rushed exodus, Mr. Barnes beckoned me to stay behind. I obediently retrieved my bag and made my way over to his desk.

"How was your inaugural year, Ms. Harris?" Mr. Barnes inquired, his voice filled with genuine interest. "It was fine, and you can call me Emma, Mr. Barnes," I replied. A warm smile graced his face as he consented to refer to me as Emma.

"Have you made arrangements for your summer project?" Mr. Barnes inquired, referring to the obligatory project that all first-year students must complete before advancing to their sophomore year. Typically, students wrote a paper about their summer experiences or crafted a video detailing a recent trip. However, my friends and I decided to establish a club and document our summer activities.

"Yes, sir. I've already secured a summer-long reservation for a room at the library, and I still have the worksheet you gave me," I informed him. He nodded in approval and added, "That's excellent. As your advisor, I want to ensure you have all the necessary resources. If you require any assistance, feel free to reach out to me through email, alright?" I reciprocated with a nod, expressing my gratitude. "Thank you, Mr. Barnes. I wish you a fantastic summer," I said as I bid him farewell. As I exited the room, Mr. Barnes waved goodbye. Now, I needed to rendezvous with Sophia and Liam to commence our summer adventures.

Navigating my way to my locker felt like maneuvering through a bustling city street during rush hour. The chaotic stream of students was like a flowing river, everyone eager to escape the school's confines. Despite the frantic rush, I needed to stop by my locker to gather a few things. The packed hallways seemed to stretch endlessly, making the journey to my locker seem like an arduous task. However, a stroke of luck revealed the stairwell, and I quickly veered off the main hallway toward the second floor.

It took some effort to push through the crowd, but I eventually made it to the stairwell. As I ascended to the second floor, the atmosphere shifted drastically from the commotion downstairs. Nevertheless, knowing that Liam and Emma were waiting for me urged me to quicken my pace. Finally reaching my locker, I swung it open to retrieve the books I needed and my computer. An unexpected sight greeted me—a mirror that I had forgotten I had put up at the beginning of the year. I had intended to use it more often, but the hustle and bustle of daily life had made me neglect it. Gazing at my reflection, I couldn't help but feel a pang of self-consciousness. My straight blond hair and fair complexion made me feel ordinary, like everyone else. The only features setting me apart were my glasses and perhaps my freckles. Feeling disheartened, I debated whether to take down the mirror. However, as I pondered, my attention was drawn to three girls in the distance – ones I preferred to avoid at all costs. I swiftly closed my locker and attempted to walk away, but they called out to me, halting my departure.

As I was about to leave, I heard someone call out, "Sophia, wait!" I turned around and saw the top three mean girls of Pine Ridge High approaching. The leader of the group was Lily Waston, a typical blond, rich girl who exuded an entitled air. Standing to her left was Ella Gray, the star player of the tennis team, whose physical resemblance and talent on the court likened her to Serena Williams. Finally, on Lily's right was Chloe Morgan, a new Hispanic girl who had quickly integrated into the popular clique due to her father's ownership of the largest car dealership in Sunnybrook, Georgia.

As Lily approached me, her perfectly styled hair and immaculate uniform contrasted sharply with my rumpled appearance. "So, are you coming to the charity dinner at the country club tonight?" she inquired, her tone laced with thinly veiled condescension.

I glanced over at Chloe and Ella, who were exchanging knowing smirks. "Well, of course, I'll be there; my mom is hosting the event," I replied, hoping to assert some sense of belonging.

Lily casually picked at my tie and remarked, "I hope you show up better than this. It's funny how the Mayor and Police Chief's daughter couldn't be bothered to look presentable. My father runs the country club, and I always make sure to uphold his standards. It's important not to tarnish his reputation, but it seems like you don't care about that." Her words stung, and I instinctively brushed her hand away, tersely informing her that I would see them tonight.

As I walked away, their laughter echoed in the distance. Maybe Lily had a point;

perhaps I should make more effort to look polished, especially given my family's position in the community. However, my dad had always emphasized the importance of staying true to myself and not getting caught up in superficial appearances. Nevertheless, a recent overheard conversation between my parents revealed my mom's desire for me to take more pride in my appearance, prompting me to begrudgingly place a mirror in my locker. As a result, that mirror had become a symbol of inner conflict, eventually being obscured by history books that provided a comforting escape into the past.

While I yearned to lose myself in historical narratives and eschew society's unwritten expectations, the reality of my parents' demanding schedules meant attending numerous social functions and dinners. Yet amidst this, the prospect of co-founding a club with Emma and Liam offered a glimmer of respite from the pressures of my social obligations. I hastened my pace, eager to start this new endeavor.

The hallways in my school are absolutely chaotic right now. It's so crowded that I've decided to just stay in the computer lab for a while. I should be on my way to meet Emma and Sophia, but with how thin I am, I feel like I'll get squished against a locker in no time. When I caught a glimpse of myself on the computer screen, I couldn't help but think that I resembled Steve Urkel from the old TV show Family Matters. This reminded me of how my dad used to make me watch classic movies and TV shows when he found out I wanted to be a director. He believed it was important for me to understand how to create magic on screen with minimal resources. He often emphasized the charm of capturing special moments without relying on the latest technology. Even though my phone has a good camera, I still long for a new camcorder. There's just something special about the weight and feel of a camera in your hands that can't be replicated by a phone.

"Liam Parker, are you still in here?" Mr. Knight, the computer teacher, walked into the empty classroom, and I could tell he was about to lock up. I explained that I was waiting for the hallway to clear out before I left. He nodded and walked over to me, taking a seat. Despite his name, Mr. Knight looked nothing like what you'd expect a knight to look. He had a substantial belly, a shiny balding head, pale white skin, and a neatly trimmed black and grey goatee. Despite his unconventional appearance, he was my favorite teacher. He always had great movie recommendations and would often suggest directors for me to study.

Curious about his summer plans, I asked Mr. Knight what he was going to do for the upcoming break. He mentioned that he and his wife were planning to go on a cruise. I laughed and told him to have a great time. He then turned the question on me, prompting me to share my own plans. I couldn't wait to tell him about the club that my friends and I were planning to start.

Over the summer, my friends Emma, Sophia, and I decided to team up and start a club for our summer project. We hadn't decided on the exact theme for the club yet, but I was thrilled to have the opportunity to spend quality time with my friends.

To be honest, I've always considered myself a bit of a nerdy outcast, struggling to make connections with others. However, things changed at the start of the year when Emma and I found ourselves in the same computer class. She caught me watching an old stop-motion movie called Clash of the Titans, and we ended up bonding through her love of mythology. It was a special moment for me, as it marked the first time I had truly connected with someone other than my dad. From that point on, Emma and I became friends, and she later introduced me to Sophia.

I was already familiar with Sophia because her dad was the police chief, and her mom was the mayor, which made her seem important, yet I had no idea she was also an outcast like me. To my surprise, Sophia was incredibly kind to me and even shared fascinating historical facts about how older movies were made. I couldn't deny that I had developed a significant crush on her, although I felt she was too beautiful and well-connected to be interested in someone like me. Regardless, I held onto the hope that perhaps things could work out, just like in the movies.

I told Mr. Knight about the club we were planning, and he wished me a happy summer before glancing at the clock.

When I followed his gaze, I realized I was running very late to meet up with Emma and Sophia. I quickly excused myself, promising to catch up with Mr. Knight later, and hastily grabbed my bag before rushing out of the room.

As I arrived at the meet-up spot in front of the school on the steps, I couldn't help but marvel at the fact that I was the first one there. We had all agreed to meet at this spot, and I had anticipated that Sophia would have beaten me to it. However, it seemed like she and Liam were caught in the stampede of students rushing to leave the school. Nevertheless, I didn't mind the wait - it gave me time to gather my thoughts for my pitch to convince them to start a mythology club.

The idea had been brewing in my mind for about a week. I envisioned a club where we would delve into the fascinating world of legends and myths, studying and unraveling their stories throughout the summer. I had already figured out everyone's roles in the club - Sophia would be our historian, capturing the rich tapestry of myths and legends, and Liam would channel his creativity as our filmmaker. As for me, I saw myself as the club's myth specialist, dedicated to unraveling the mysteries of these timeless tales.

We all have our roles, and I think they would work perfectly for the club. A second later, Sophia showed up behind me, apologizing for being late. I told her it was fine. "I'm looking forward to starting this club. I hope it can get my mind off of this dinner I have to go to tonight," Sophia said. She looked sad, and I knew she hated going to social events, but she had to because of who her mom was. "It's going to be okay. After we have so much fun, you will need that boring dinner to cool yourself down," I said. We both laughed, and she asked me where Liam was. I told her he probably lost track of time. Sophia turned back to the school doors, saying that she hoped he was okay. "Oh, are you worried your boyfriend got lost?" I teased. Sophia's face turned bright red, and she spun towards me and told me to shut up. I laughed, and I could tell she was trying to calm herself down.

As Liam arrived, he appeared to be out of breath, as though he had just finished running a marathon. "Sorry for being late. I had to navigate through the stampede in the hallway," he explained. Understanding the situation, Sophia and I nodded in response. Liam expressed his excitement about the school year coming to an end and eagerly anticipated the start of summer. Teasingly, I remarked, "With your luck, I'm surprised you weren't late for summer." This prompted a smirk from Liam, who responded, "I've only been late maybe five times; that's not a big deal." In good spirits, we laughed, and I playfully added, "Five is still more than one." Liam seemed to be on the verge of protest until Sophia interjected, urging us to focus.

"So, I have an idea for our club," I said, eagerly looking at Liam and Sophia. They both encouraged me to share, so I began explaining how I envisioned our club delving deeper into mythology and exploring the rich tapestry of legends and myths throughout history. I suggested that Sophia could take on the role of our historian, sharing insights into the cultural backgrounds of the myths we discuss. I also proposed that Liam could be our filmmaker, capturing our exploration and turning it into a compelling docuseries. As for myself, I saw my role as the myth specialist, ensuring that we always have captivating topics to discuss and sharing the stories behind them.

There was a moment of silence after I finished speaking, and in my mind, I feared that my friends might not be keen on the idea. But to my surprise, Liam expressed his excitement, saying, "I love that idea, especially since I get to film something." Sophia also chimed in, sharing her enthusiasm, "I have so many cultural books at my house. I can delve into the historical background of whichever story we're exploring. This idea brings together all of our interests so that no one feels left out. What a wonderful idea, Emma," she said with a smile.

Their positive response left me overjoyed. "I was worried you guys wouldn't like it," I confessed. Liam patted me on the shoulder and said, "You had me at filmmaker." We all shared a moment of laughter, and it was clear from Sophia's beaming smile that my idea had struck a chord with both of them.

With the laughter subsiding, Sophia brought up the topic of our uniform fatigue. She suggested that we should return to our respective homes, change into casual clothes, and gather any necessary items for the club. Both Liam and I agreed with her proposal. I mentioned that I had unintentionally left my laptop at home, adding to our list of preparations. We decided to regroup at the library once we had everything we needed so that we could officially kick off the club. With a nod from Sophia and Liam, we made our way to the bike rack, retrieved our bicycles, and bid each other farewell as we rode towards our respective houses.

Chapter 2
Home Sweet Home

As I pedaled along on my bike, I couldn't help but ponder whether my dad would be back home. I could almost picture him asking, "Emma, why are you home from school so early?" It seemed like he hardly paid any attention to me these days, so I doubted he'd remember my early dismissal today. Pulling up to our house, I scanned the driveway for his beloved red Thunderbird. Sometimes I wondered if he loved that car more than he loved me. Coming to a stop at the top of the driveway, I gazed up at the familiar sight of our house, feeling a mix of uncertainty and longing.

Our quaint little home always struck me as amusing, considering my own rather eccentric nature. It was a charming single-story house topped with a vibrant red metal roof and adorned with a cheerful yellow exterior. Encircling the entire property was a small, weathered wooden fence, further enhancing its cozy appeal. The lush green lawn provided the perfect backdrop to the house's inviting facade. On the front porch, neglected potted plants stood as a silent testament to their lack of care.

After my mom lost her battle with cancer last year, the burden of tending to the plants fell upon me and my father. However, both of us struggled to find the motivation to care for them. It was heartbreaking to see the plants wilting, reminding us of the absence of my mom's nurturing touch. I never had the same knack for gardening that my mom did, and my dad was preoccupied with his responsibilities as a fire chief, using work as a means to avoid confronting his emotions and distancing himself from me. While I had a strong bond with my mom, my relationship with my dad became strained, and some days it felt like we were mere acquaintances.

I opened the front door, stepped into the living room, and saw my dad sitting on the worn-out couch surrounded by stacks of paperwork. His brow furrowed in concentration as he hunched over the cluttered coffee table. I coughed to announce my presence, and finally, he glanced up, a faint look of surprise crossing his face.

"Why are you home so early?" he asked, his voice tinged with confusion. I took a deep breath, already knowing that he had forgotten our early release for the last day of school.

"Dad, it's the last day of school, remember? We got out early today," I reminded him gently. He nodded absentmindedly and returned his gaze to the papers spread out in front of him. I hesitated for a moment before deciding to engage with him.

My father was an imposing figure, towering over six feet tall, with a muscular build earned through dedicated workouts. His frame was so substantial that finding a well-fitting shirt was always a challenge. Like me, he had dark skin, but his face was largely concealed behind his thick, striking black and grey beard.

"What are you working on, Dad?" I inquired, trying to spark a conversation. He met my gaze briefly and muttered, "Just some budget stuff," before his eyes drifted back to the paperwork.

I sensed his disinterest and awkwardly shifted on my feet. "Hey, Dad, remember I told you about the club me and my friends are starting? I'm going to change and head to the library," I said, hoping to draw his attention. He gave a distracted nod and mumbled, "Go have fun," without looking up.

Feeling deflated, I glanced down at the floor and quietly retreated to my room, the unspoken distance between us hanging heavy in the air.

As I strolled down the hallway, I couldn't help but notice the pictures of my mom adorning the walls. The resemblance between us was uncanny, although her hair was sleeker and her complexion a touch lighter than mine. Her beauty was undeniable, and it was perplexing to acknowledge that we shared similar features. Yet, it was her radiant smile that truly set her apart. Her smile exuded warmth and had the power to illuminate an entire room, instantly garnering trust and admiration. Meeting someone as genuinely kind as her seemed improbable. Her boundless compassion often made me wonder if she was truly human.

I remember how my fascination with mythology began. It all started with my mom, who used to tell me captivating stories about Hercules and his 13 adventures when I was a child. Her storytelling ignited a deep curiosity within me to delve into the world of mythology and explore the diverse stories and legends that different cultures have to offer. Despite my unconventional interest, my mom was always incredibly supportive, never questioning my passion. I often find myself dreaming of emulating the heroes from those ancient stories, but I'm unsure of how to even begin. Perhaps, someday, I will discover the path to making that dream a reality.

I entered my bedroom, which served as my sanctuary. My bed was positioned against the window, framed by posters of fantastical creatures and brave heroes. On my nightstand, I proudly displayed a minotaur and a griffin statue that I had acquired from a vibrant art festival in town. The towering stacks of books, reaching almost up to the ceiling, stood as a testament to my love for stories that filled my heart but seemed to escape my grasp due to lack of time. Feeling the need for change, I glanced at my reflection in the mirror, realizing Sophia was right about the school uniforms being quite dreary.

I made my way to the closet and picked out a pair of well-worn ripped jeans and a black t-shirt featuring my favorite band, Black Sabbath. Heavy metal was my jam, even though my dad had hoped I'd prefer something more in line with Taylor Swift. Grabbing my laptop, which had found a temporary resting spot on the bean bag chair in the corner, I packed it in my backpack before finally leaving my room.

As I reached the front door, I hesitated, wanting to exchange a few words with my dad, but he was engrossed in his work and didn't look up. A wave of melancholy swept over me, but I shook it off and stepped outside. I opted to leave my bike behind and set off on foot, knowing that the park and library were within a quick ten-minute walk from our house.

As I approached my house, a strange sensation always washed over me. I parked my bike by the front gate and strolled up the driveway. The architecture and grandeur of the house seemed more suited to someone like Lily Watson, with her glamorous style, rather than a history nerd like me, Sophia Cook. It almost felt like the kind of house a mayor's family would live in. Well, I mean, we are the mayor's family.

The house was truly stunning. It was a majestic 2-story white residence with a striking black roof. The grand porch at the front was adorned with magnificent white pillars, and a charming white fence gracefully surrounded the front of the property. A delightful pool house with a modest grey roof and a classic chimney was nestled at the back of the house, catching the eye of passersby. The front of the house featured large windows adorned with contrasting black shutters, which beautifully offset the radiant white exterior. The entrance was a focal point, marked by a bold, oversized red door flanked by charming small windows on either side.

As a history enthusiast, one can appreciate the historical charm of the house with its vintage appeal. However, for someone like me, I find myself more inclined to admire its aesthetics from afar rather than inhabit its space. Being the mayor's daughter brought an overwhelming amount of attention that I never sought. This constant scrutiny made me feel like I was trapped, always under the watchful eye of the public, expected to maintain a flawless image. The reality, though, is that I am an introvert and prefer solitude. I never sought the company of large crowds, yet I was constantly thrust into social situations against my will.

I opened the heavy wooden door and ascended the creaky stairs to my room, hoping to avoid my parents if they returned home. They never really understood me. Despite my preference for blending into the crowd, they always pushed me to the forefront. My parents were an ideal pair, both thriving in the spotlight. My mother's unwavering passion for politics led her to become the perfect fit for the role of mayor, while my father, driven to instigate change, worked tirelessly to rise to the rank of police captain. They complemented each other beautifully, supporting and aiding each other in reaching their goals. While I admired their synergy, their insistence on imposing their aspirations upon me made me long to retreat into my shell, akin to a turtle seeking refuge.

I've never been one to seek out the limelight, but I have always had a deep fascination with other people's interests and backgrounds. While I have been reticent to discuss my own story, I have always relished learning about others. As I grew up, I found myself delving into the lives of extraordinary individuals throughout history and their unique backgrounds. Exploring someone's history and the culture from which they emerged has always ignited my curiosity. I vividly recall attending a cultural event at the library dedicated to Native American heritage, and I was captivated by the deep and profound history of that culture. It opened up a whole new world for me, and I yearned to delve deeper into it. Perhaps one day, I will have the opportunity to travel the world and visit the places that have captured my imagination in my readings. But for now, I'll content myself with dreaming about those adventures.

As I turned the doorknob and pushed open the door to my room, I was greeted by the familiar sight of my personal sanctuary. The simple, unembellished nature of the room is exactly what draws me to it. The hardwood floors provide a robust and earthy foundation, while a vibrant red rug sits proudly in the center, adding a pop of color and warmth to the space. Against one wall, two intricately engraved bookshelves stand as proud sentinels, adorned with an extensive collection of books reflecting diverse cultures and historical events in the United States.

In the corner of the room, my bed is snugly pressed against a large window, which offers a beautiful view of the pool outside. I cherish the calming and invigorating moments I spend swimming, especially on scorching hot days. However, a sense of frustration creeps in when my mom hosts her campaign pool parties, disrupting the tranquility of my personal oasis.

I turned to the closest and looked for my blue summer dress to set out for dinner later tonight. However, as I rummaged through my closet, my eyes fell upon my favorite pair of blue jeans and a soft, plain white T-shirt. As I reached for them, I remembered that I had to pack my backpack for the library. I emptied out my backpack, removed all the school supplies, and carefully packed my laptop, a few snacks, and a water bottle. With my bag slung over my shoulder, I headed downstairs and stepped out the front door. I hopped onto my bike and began the tranquil ride to the library.

The journey back home on my bike was always a bit of a struggle. Although my house wasn't far, the ride involved tackling a steep hill that left my legs burning. Despite all the effort I put into that hill, I was still known as the guy with the skinny legs at school rather than "Liam, the man with legs of steel," as one might have expected. Upon reaching the top of the hill, my house, a simple blue structure with a brown roof, stood to the right.

It wasn't extravagant—just a one-story house with a small porch that didn't offer much space for relaxation. However, there was something unique about it—the attic. Situated on top of the house, the attic had a large window that made it look like a miniature house perched atop the main building. This was my room, a space I moved into after my father's tragic passing in a car accident a year ago.

His absence left a void, and life hasn't been the same since. While my mom and sister had each other, I often felt isolated. They shared similar interests and got along well, but they didn't quite understand me the way my dad did. He always supported and understood me, encouraging me to pursue my dreams.

I vividly recall the day we watched "Mrs. Doubtfire" together, and it wasn't the actors that captured my interest, but rather the direction of the film and the emotions it evoked. Inspired, I shared with my dad my aspiration to become a director, and he couldn't have been more thrilled. He went above and beyond to nurture my passion, even collecting old DVDs and VHS tapes to explore the art of filmmaking together. He worked as a manager in the local movie theater, and I cherished the opportunity to watch the latest releases with him. It brought him immense joy to see me aspire to join the film industry, but I deeply wish he were still here to guide me. I miss him every day, and I hope he knows that.

As I opened the front door, I saw my older sister, Charlotte, sitting on the couch in the living room. She had a striking appearance, reminiscent of someone from a 1980s crime show, with a big afro adorned with a purple bandana wrapped around her forehead. Her outfit was unconventional for lounging at home - a vibrant red blouse paired with leather skinny jeans. It was clear that she was dressed to go out rather than just relaxing at home.

As I tried to quietly make my way to my room, Charlotte called out to me, "Hey, are you just going to walk by without saying hello?" I returned her greeting and attempted to continue on my way, but she seemed determined to engage in conversation. "What are you up to?" she inquired, peering over the pages of a fashion magazine. Reluctantly, I mentioned that I was planning to meet my friends at the library.

"You mean those two losers that you hang out with; you need to find some better friends, Liam." She said. I got really angry and told her to never speak about my friends like that again. She responded with,

"Oh, I'm sorry if the truth hurts. But if you ever want to be popular like me, you need to upgrade. It shouldn't be that hard. Mom owns the most popular café in town. Everyone comes by our place after school to hang out. But what do you do? You go up to the attic and watch your old movies like a hermit. You know what, go ahead and be a loser. It doesn't affect me anyway." Charlotte then went back to reading her magazine. I was so furious, but I decided to just go up to my room so I wouldn't have to see her.

I climbed up to the attic and turned the doorknob to my bedroom. As I stepped inside, I noticed the simple layout of the room. A twin-sized bed rested on the floor, and beside it, a bookshelf stood beneath the window. The shelves were filled with dusty VHS tapes and DVDs. Next to the bookshelf, my desk held my computer, the centerpiece of my filmmaking area. I've spent countless hours here creating short documentaries showcasing the beauty of Sunnybrook, Georgia. Despite my passion, I never found the courage to share my films with my friends, feeling a sense of embarrassment. However, I hold onto the hope that one day, I'll create a movie that captures the hearts of many.

As I glanced down at my drab school uniform, I couldn't help but feel a sense of disdain. In one swift motion, I shed the uniform and slipped into a simple red t-shirt and khaki shorts. My school supplies were carelessly scattered on the bed as I grabbed my laptop. Across the room, my Dad's old camcorder caught my eye. It had been a birthday gift from him two years ago, but I hadn't really used it much. However, for this project, I thought the vintage touch of an old video camera might be just what we needed as we delved into the realm of ancient myths over the summer. With that in mind, I stashed the camcorder in my bag and made my way downstairs.

Before stepping out the door, I turned to my sister, who was still seated on the couch, and expressed my thoughts, "I'd rather have genuine friends who truly care about me than hang out with superficial, popular friends who only stick around for the free treats at Mom's café." Without waiting for her response, I exited through the front door, closing it firmly behind me.

I strolled down the driveway, feeling the gravel crunch under my feet, and then hopped back onto my bike. The descent down the hill was exhilarating compared to the uphill struggle. The wind rushed past me as I coasted down, and I couldn't help but think about all the amazing adventures the upcoming summer held. At the same time, a small voice inside me reminded me that I needed to pick up the pace or risk being late.

Chapter 3
Starting A New Club

As I strolled through the park, I felt a sense of calm wash over me with each step I took. Oakwood Park, conveniently located right next to my house, had become my sanctuary. The gentle breeze caressed my face while the warm sunlight enveloped me, revitalizing my spirit. The park's natural beauty, with squirrels rustling in the trees and birds flitting from branch to branch, provided a serene escape from the hustle and bustle of town life.

To my left, the joyful laughter of children echoed through the air, marking the end of their school day. As I continued to walk, I couldn't help but smile, feeling a twinge of envy at their carefree delight. A crystal-clear pond adorned the park, allowing a glimpse of the tranquil pond floor. The distant sounds of ducks splashing in the water filled the air, drawing my attention to a mother duck leading her adorable ducklings. Witnessing this tender sight stirred bittersweet memories of my own mother.

Nestled near the pond was a peculiar yet beloved sight. Standing resolute was a striking statue of Athena, the ancient Greek goddess of wisdom, adorned with an owl perched on one shoulder, a book cradled in one arm, and a sword gripping the other. I had always been drawn to Athena, admiring her trademark resourcefulness and intelligence in Greek mythology. Despite its unexpectedness, the presence of this statue in the park brought me great joy.

I hurried to the library to avoid being late; the park lay just next to the Maple Grove Library, a place that felt like a second home to me. I often found myself there, as it was just a short stroll through the park from my house. As I neared the library, its grand appearance never failed to impress me.

The Maple Grove Library, a treasured historical site nestled in the heart of Sunnybrook, Georgia, has a rich legacy as a hub for diverse educational pursuits. The library stands tall, encompassing three magnificent stories, and is crafted from re-splendent, crimson bricks that exude time-less grandeur. Its majestic roof is crowned with magnificent jade hawk sculptures nestled at each corner, casting an entranc-ing emerald glow that beautifully con-trasts the rich brick exterior. Enveloping the building are expansive, oval-shaped windows fashioned from sleek green glass, which seamlessly harmonize with the ver-dant roof, presenting a truly enchanting and idyllic spectacle for all who gaze upon it.

As I strolled across the bustling street, the library loomed ahead, its imposing fa-cade drawing me in. Climbing the stone steps, I was greeted by the imposing wood-en doors. Before I ventured into the heart of the library, I paused at the small, welcoming room where the librarian, Ms. Reed, presided behind an oak desk framed by shelves of antique books. Ms. Reed, a woman in her late fifties, exuded an air of authority with her elegant blond-gray hair and fair, almost porcelain-like complexion. Adorned with old-fashioned spectacles, she embodied the quintessential librarian look.

"Hello, Ms. Reed. How are you today?" I asked, approaching the desk. She smiled warmly and assured me that she was feeling quite well before inquiring whether I had come to check out my room. Confirming this, I asked if it was still reserved for the entire summer.

"The room is indeed reserved for you, dear. Just be sure to abide by the guidelines. Here's the code to your room: 1949, and the room number is 315," Ms. Reed confirmed with a kind nod. Expressing my gratitude, I made my way into the library.

The library's central area was designed with an open layout, allowing visitors to see all the levels from the ground floor. The skylight flooded the space with natural light, negating the need for additional lighting. The ground floor housed the children's section, but it also served as the gateway to the second and third floors. Access to the upper levels was available either through stairs or the elevator. Despite being designated for children, the ground floor was expansive and impressive. Parents and children wandered around, selecting books from the shelves and reading at uniquely shaped tables. As I made my way to the elevator, I couldn't help but smile at the kids I passed.

I was aware that the second floor housed the majority of the library's book collection, while the third floor housed both books and various office and study rooms. About three weeks ago, I made a reservation for an office room for the entire summer. As I entered the elevator, I specifically pressed the button for the third floor.

I stepped into the elevator and pressed the button for the third floor. As the elevator doors opened, I was greeted by the split-floor layout. In the center, there was an open area with railings to prevent anyone from falling over the ledge. To one side, there were rows of bookshelves, while the other side was lined with office doors and study rooms.

I made my way towards the office area, passing by numerous doors and peeking through windows to catch glimpses of people in meetings and students immersed in their studies. After a bit of searching, I arrived at room 315. I entered the code 1949 on the keypad and heard a satisfying click. With the door unlocked, I stepped inside.

The room was quite ordinary, yet spacious and inviting. As I entered, my eyes were immediately drawn to the large window on the right side, offering a panoramic view of the city skyline. In the center of the room, a substantial rectangular table stood, surrounded by comfortable chairs. The back wall was unadorned, creating a sense of openness and simplicity, while the opposite wall featured a vast whiteboard that extended the entire length. Taking a seat, I pulled out my laptop and opened the worksheet outlining the guidelines for our summer project. Leaning back in my chair, I couldn't help but ponder over what the upcoming summer held in store for me. Despite feeling a mix of nerves and excitement about the project, I was eager to hang out with my friends.

Just as the room fell silent, the door swung open, and in walked Liam and Sophia, their voices mingling in a discussion about their favorite cookies. "Chocolate chip is clearly the superior choice," Liam declared confidently. "No way, peanut butter cookies are the best. Peanut butter is not only delicious but also a healthier option," Sophia countered. Liam chuckled, adding, "But let's not forget they both have sugar, so can we really call them healthy snacks?" Sophia maintained her stance, saying, "Despite the sugar content, peanut butter cookies are still a better choice than chocolate chip." As they settled into the room, Liam suggested, "I think we should settle this debate by going out later and getting some cookies." Sophia blushed at the unexpected invitation and busied herself with the whiteboard to avoid eye contact. Liam, oblivious to the impact of his words, took a seat by the window while Sophia glanced furtively in his direction, hoping he would understand the unspoken proposal for a cookie date.

To break the awkward atmosphere of the situation, I suggested starting the meeting. "Now that we've clarified our roles in the club, we still need to decide on a club name," I remarked. Sophia volunteered to write down the suggestions on the whiteboard so that we could choose later. Both Liam and I agreed to this approach. Liam suggested that we focus on mythology for the club name. I asked Liam if he should start recording for the film, but he decided to wait until we had finalized all the details. He pointed out that we hadn't selected which story we were going to discuss or decided on the theme for the first episode. I agreed, acknowledging that he was right. Meanwhile, Sophia was patiently waiting for us to come up with names. Liam and I enthusiastically began shouting out names while Sophia diligently wrote them down. After brainstorming, we came up with the following potential names: Mythology Master, Legendary Lore Club, Ancient Legend League, Mythos Explorers, Mythology Enthusiasts, Fables & Folklore Fellowship, Mythical Mind Club, Pantheon Pursuits, Epic Tales Guild, Mythical Marvels Society, Divine Myths Club, Heroes & Gods Club, Saga Scholars, and finally Mythic Journeys Club.

None of the names seemed quite fitting until Sophia came up with a suggestion. "How about the Myth Hunter Society?" she offered. Both Liam and I exchanged glances and simultaneously exclaimed, "That's the perfect name!" Sophia was visibly surprised by our immediate agreement. I encouraged her to speak up more often. A smile spread across Sophia's face as she wrote the new club name on the board.

"Now that we've settled on our name, I think it's time for some thorough research. We should each go and explore books relevant to our respective roles in the club. I'm planning to peruse the Ancient History section of the library to unearth more stories for us to discuss." Liam expressed his intention to browse through the film and music department in search of inspiration for our project. Meanwhile, Sophia decided to delve into the cultural history department to gather more information about the origins of these stories. After our discussion, we all dispersed with the plan to reconvene in twenty minutes. As Sophia and Liam hurried out, I lingered for a moment, gazing out the window and feeling reassured that everything was under control.

Chapter 4

Everything Goes Dark

After reaching the second floor, Sophia and I went our separate ways. She made her way to the history section while I set out to find the film section. It seemed that Emma had stayed behind as she hadn't joined us. The library was vast, and despite having been there only a few times before, this visit felt different. The towering rows of books were almost imposing, creating a sense of awe. Venturing into the film section was a first for me, and I was curious to explore the rumored movie artifacts. Following the signs, I found myself walking through other sections, such as the fine art department and the poetry department.

As I made my way through the library, I was captivated by the attention to detail in each department. Each section had its own area walled off by bookshelves and the library wall. The fine arts section, in particular, left me speechless with its breathtaking artwork and murals adorning the walls. The poetry area welcomed me with its cozy seating, creating a serene atmosphere for reading and contemplation. Meanwhile, the vibrant paint section for kids buzzed with youthful energy as children excitedly experimented with colors and brushes. Following the signage to the film section led me to a long, grand hallway, where multiple arrows pointed toward different sections, adding an air of mystery and exploration to the journey. Finally reaching the film section, I eagerly continued my exploration of the library's diverse and intriguing offerings.

As I made my way down a long hallway, my mind was filled with determination. I had a big responsibility to fulfill, as Sophia and Emma were relying on me. This was my first time directing and filming a docuseries, and I was adamant about not letting them down. The challenge was significant, considering I only had a cheap 2012 camcorder and editing software that I received as a birthday gift a few years ago. With a budget of $0, I was on a mission to seek out books or old tapes that could provide guidance on creating movies with minimal resources. Finally, as I continued down the hallway, the film section came into view, and my excitement and determination grew stronger.

As I entered the room, the doorway immediately caught my attention. It was adorned with a film reel that elegantly wrapped around it, setting the stage for the cinematic wonderland within. The walls were adorned with posters of iconic movies from various eras, offering a visual journey through the history of film. Classic filmmaking equipment such as film reels and clapperboards added an authentic touch to the decor, while a captivating timeline mural on one wall showcased significant milestones in film history.

In one corner, a viewing area beckoned with its comfortable vintage-style theater chairs, inviting visitors to relax and immerse themselves in the world of cinema. Nearby, a small screening area featured a projector and a screen, poised to transport viewers into the realms of classic films. As I explored further, I discovered a treasure trove of knowledge on film history, with bookshelves filled with books delving into the industry's evolution, biographies of famous filmmakers, and classic screenplays waiting to be explored.

I spent some time searching through the bookshelf, hoping to discover books focused on creating films with limited budgets. After sifting through the stacks, I eventually found what I was looking for at the bottom of the shelf. I uncovered "Rebel Without a Crew: Or How a 23-Year-Old Filmmaker with $7,000 Became a Hollywood Player" by Robert Rodriguez, "The Filmmaker's Handbook: A Comprehensive Guide for the Digital Age" by Steven Ascher and Edward Pincus, and "Making Movies on Your Own: Practical Tips from the Trenches" by Matt Stoller and Matt Stoller Zeitz. I can't wait to dig into these books. I think they'll give me some great ideas for my filmmaking goals.

I grabbed my books and made my way back to the third floor. As I walked, I was certain that I would be the last person to return. It seemed like I was always late when we had to meet up. I always tried my best, but for some reason, I always seemed to run out of time. I made it back to the stairs, doing my best to stay out of people's way. The library was packed with people. I had never really enjoyed the library before, but I think that changed when I discovered the amazing film room.

When I got to our clubroom, it was empty. I was relieved to not be the last one for once. I set my books down and waited for Emma and Sophia to come back. I still wonder why Sophia reacted so strangely when I suggested getting cookies. Oh, wa it... did I accidentally ask her out on a date?

As Liam and I parted ways, I headed towards the history department. My task was to delve into the background of the myth we were about to unravel. Although I was somewhat familiar with the layout of the library, the section housing cultural history was uncharted territory for me. As I wandered through the department, I realized that the history section was diverse, encompassing political, social, economic, and military history and more. Turning a corner, I spotted a librarian and approached her for directions. "Hi, my name is Sophia. I'm looking for the Cultural History section. Can you point me in the right direction?" The librarian smiled and directed me to the Religious History section, which was adjacent to my destination. I thanked her and made my way there.

I took a left turn from the Religious History section and entered an expansive open-floor area dedicated to cultural history. The walls were adorned with stunning murals depicting scenes from various historical periods. Display cases showcased an array of fascinating artifacts, such as tools, jewelry, and other culturally significant items. It was captivating to see flags and traditional clothing from diverse parts of the world. The shelves were meticulously organized by region, and there was a prominent display stand featuring the latest books on historical culture.

I spent some time browsing through bookshelves, carefully selecting a book from each culture that would provide valuable insights for our project. I came across "A History of Ancient Greece in Fifty Lives" by David Stuttard, "The Viking World" by James Graham-Campbell, "The Oxford History of Ancient Egypt" by Ian Shaw, "The Ramayana" by

R.K. Narayan, "Celtic Myths and Legends" by Peter Berresford Ellis, "A History of Africa" by John Reader, and lastly, "Native American Myths and Legends" by Richard Erdoes and Alfonso Ortiz.

I made my way back to the third floor with all the books I had collected. Carrying them was no easy task, and I found myself trying my best not to walk into anyone as I made my way through the building. With my hands full, I couldn't even consider taking the elevator, so I carefully ascended the stairs, one step at a time. Once I reached the third floor and approached our room, I caught sight of Liam through the window. I knocked on the door with my shoe to get his attention, and he opened the door to let me in. Liam immediately noticed the multitude of books I was carrying and offered to help. I grateful-ly accepted, and together, we set the books down on the table.

I sank into the chair, letting out a long exhale. The weight of the books I'd been lugging around hit me all at once, and I suddenly felt utterly worn out. Liam set-tled into a seat across from me, but there was something different about him today. He seemed fidgety, his eyes kept darting away, and then he mumbled, "Hey Sophia, about earlier when I mentioned going to grab some cookies later..." My heart started racing as I anticipated what he might say next. Did he want to ask me out? I had hesitated the first time he asked, feeling too shy to respond, and now here he was, bringing it up again. What should I do? Should I say yes? Or would that change everything between us? No, I should listen to him first. "I, uh, I just wanted to say that I didn't really think about it before, but I'd like to take you if you're interested," he stammered. I was completely caught off guard, but before I could gather my words, Emma burst into the room, clutching an enormous, weathered book in her hands.

As I stood in the clubroom, I decided to let Sophia and Liam go ahead of me so that I could carefully consider which books I wanted to grab. It was important to me that we found the right books for each cul-ture. After a moment of contemplation, I realized that I couldn't linger forever, so I left the clubroom and descended the stairs, heading toward the history department.

Navigating the familiar halls, I made my way to the mythology section, a place that always felt like a second home to me. Along the way, I spotted Sophia engaged in conversation with a librarian. I couldn't help but wonder if she had gotten lost, but it seemed like she had found her way. I continued on, feeling drawn to the mythology section, almost as if it was calling my name. I had checked out most of the books in this section before, so the librarians should be familiar with my name, Emma. After a little more walking, I finally arrived at the mythology section, ready to explore and find the perfect books.

The room was enclosed by towering wooden bookshelves, creating a sense of grandeur and enclosure. A captivating mural adorned the back wall, displaying vibrant scenes from various myths, including the Greek gods on Mount Olympus and the Norse gods in Asgard. The area was adorned with statues of prominent deities such as Zeus, Thor, and Anubis, contributing to the room's immersive ambiance. Decorative banners and posters featuring symbols like the Greek laurel wreath, the Norse Yggdrasil (World Tree), and the Celtic triskelion added to the rich tapestry of cultural influences. The seating options were carefully crafted to resemble ancient thrones, exuding an air of regality and comfort. In one corner, there was a charming and intimate nook designed to resemble a mystical cave, inviting visitors to immerse themselves in the enchanting atmosphere.

As soon as I remembered the books I wanted, I hurried over to the bookshelves. After a bit of searching, I managed to find nearly all of them. I was excited to pick up "Norse Mythology" by Neil Gaiman, "Egyptian Mythology: A Guide to the Gods, Goddesses, and Traditions of Ancient Egypt" by Geraldine Pinch, "The Ramayana" by R.K. Narayan, "Chinese Mythology: An Introduction" by Anne Birrell, and finally "African Myths of Origin" by Stephen Belcher.

I carefully placed my stack of books on a nearby table. As I surveyed the room, a feeling of uncertainty crept over me. It was as if someone's eyes were fixed on me, sending a shiver down my spine. Slowly turning around, I found myself alone in the room. However, an inexplicable pull drew my attention to a shadowy corner of the bookshelf. There, almost hidden from view, was a solitary book, beckoning me with an inexplicable allure. As I approached, I realized it was an immense, weighty volume, bound in weathered leather and secured with thick straps. The cover, marred by deep cracks, hinted at its age and storied past. Retrieving the book from its resting place, I struggled to discern its contents in the dim light. With some effort, I deciphered Latin script adorning the cover. Fortunately, my fluency in Latin allowed me to decipher the words. The language had captivated me for years, and I had devoted countless hours to mastering it.

I ran my hand across the cover and examined the faded wording closely. I could just make out the title ***"Liber Cerberi,"*** which translates to "Book of Cerberus." Despite my efforts, I couldn't see who the author was through the cracks. Despite having just collected some other books, I felt compelled to take this one with me. As I walked away from the mythology section, I found it hard to divert my eyes from the book. I was so engrossed that I nearly bumped into people on my way back to our clubroom. Even though I had visited that section numerous times before, I had never seen this book. It had a hypnotic effect on me, and I felt a strange connection to it. I couldn't resist the feeling it stirred inside me. As I ascended the stairs, I suddenly felt light-headed, and the room seemed to darken. I heard my name being called out, almost as if it was coming from the book itself.

"...Emma...."

"....Emma, keep going. You're almost there..."

I shook myself out of it, and the light returned to the room. What was that? It must have been my imagination, but I found myself back in front of the club-room door.

I opened the door and saw Liam and Sophia in the middle of a conversation. I hoped I hadn't interrupted anything important. "What's that book in your hand?" Liam asked as he and Sophia both stood up. I walked over to the table, set the book down, and said, "I don't know, but it's called the Book of Cerberus."

We gathered around the mysterious book. Sophia remarked that she had never seen a book quite like this one, while Liam mentioned that he had seen similar books in old movies such as "The Lord of the Rings." As Liam leaned in for a closer look, he shook his head in confusion, admitting that he could not make sense of the strange symbols on the cover. I explained that it was Latin, and the only part I could read was that the book is named the Book of Cerberus.

"Have you opened it yet?" Sophia asked eagerly. I hesitated, sharing the unsettling feeling I had experienced in the mythology section earlier - it felt as though the book itself had been watching me. Their skeptical expressions made me keep quiet about the eerie encounter I'd had on the stairs. "Shall we open it, then?" Liam prodded, oblivious to my apprehension. Despite my misgivings, I reluctantly agreed, feeling an inexplicable sense of foreboding as if something was warning me to put the book back.

"Yeah, let's see what's inside; maybe it'll help with the project," Sophia suggested, seemingly unaffected by the strange vibes I was getting. I couldn't shake the feeling that something wasn't right, but I reasoned that it was just a book - what harm could possibly come from opening it?

As I opened the book to what I assumed was a random page, an inexplicable coldness pervaded the room, sending a shiver down Liam's spine. "Why did it suddenly get so cold?" he asked, visibly trembling and rubbing his arms. "Perhaps the air conditioning malfunctioned, causing the temperature to drop," Sophia suggested. However, as she spoke, I noticed her breath forming a chilling mist in the air, unlike the typical effect of cold breath on a winter day. It seemed as though more than just warmth was escaping from her body. Glancing at Liam, I observed the same phenomenon. Puzzled, I voiced my concern about the timing of the temperature drop coinciding with my opening of the book. Liam brushed it off as a coincidence, but I couldn't shake off the feeling of unease. Sophia proposed that we continue reading the book, but Liam hesitated. As they stood on either side of me, I mustered the courage to look down at the book, only to be met with a disquieting sight.

The page I opened the book to reveal a startlingly vivid drawing. The aged yellow pages served as a stark backdrop, intensifying the impact of the unsettling image. In the illustration, a dog with not one but three heads leaped out at me. The central head bore into me with its piercing, glowing yellow eyes, surrounded by a haunting reddish hue. Its visage was weathered, resembling aged leather, and it boasted shaggy black fur as dark as the deepest abyss. Short, pointed ears jutted from its head, crowned with stubby horns akin to those of a young goat. Its jaw, far from typical, housed a mouth full of elongated fangs that extended beyond its jaws, creating a malevolent, unsettling grin. The dual heads on the left and right appeared to be focused on Sophia and Liam, a confounding detail considering it was merely a drawing, yet it exuded a strikingly lifelike quality. The three-headed dog was positioned in front of a towering gate, emanating an aura of dread as though it harbored a menacing secret that should never be unveiled.

"Sophia, Liam, are you guys seeing this?" They seemed frozen in space. They didn't move or acknowledge that I had just asked a question. I touched Sophia's hand, but it was so cold it felt like it burned my hand. I tried to touch Liam, but it did the same thing. Questions swirled in my head about what was happening, but then I heard the voice again.

"....Emma..."

"...Read the words, Emma..."

"....Set me free, Emma...."

"....Release me, Emma...."

Fear struck me as the voice faded. I had no clue what was happening or why Liam and Sophia were now frozen, and only I could move. But the voice wanted me to read something. Under the drawing of the dog was a single word in Latin that I knew, but I didn't want to read it. But soon, the voice returned.

"....Emma, read aloud...."

"...Set me free...."

"...Now, Emma...."

"EMMA, READ NOW"

The voice screamed in my head, making me fall over on top of the book. A ringing noise was now blasting in my head causing me not to focus. I wanted it to stop. I screamed out, "Please stop, I'm begging you." The sound was now like nails raking across a chalkboard. The voice is even louder now.

"READ NOW OR YOUR FRIENDS WILL...."

It didn't finish, as if it knew I would know what it meant. I stood back over the book, trying to focus past the painful noise in my head. I looked at the word below the dog and repeated: ***"Emittere"*** (release).

All three of the dogs' heads on the page turned and looked at me, each with a sinister grin on their face. Suddenly, the whole room went dark.

Chapter 5

Finding Our Way Home

I couldn't believe my eyes when I witnessed Emma swinging down to the second floor like Tarzan. But that was just the beginning. Next, I saw her standing in a whirlwind of green smoke, and I couldn't make sense of what was happening. I immediately grabbed Sophia's hand, preparing to react. "Is that really Emma down there?" Sophia asked, bewildered. "Yes, but it looks like she's gained some kind of power," I responded. Suddenly, Emma got to her feet and raced toward us. I tried to signal her about the yellow-eyed people, but she seemed oblivious to my warnings. It was clear that she had a plan, and we needed to be prepared. I instructed Sophia to get ready to move, and we both stood up, ready for whatever was coming our way.

Emma dashed toward us with incredible speed, her determined expression catching my attention. The yellow-eyed people seemed to have spotted her as well, quickly redirecting their focus towards her. Despite their attempts to intercept her, she showed no signs of slowing down. As she drew nearer, I glanced at Sophia and saw the same question in her eyes as in mine - what was Emma planning to do?

As Emma approached, the first wave of yellow-eyed people charged at her, seemingly on a collision course. Just as they were about to make contact, a remarkable thing happened. The yellow-eyed figures were forcefully repelled backward, crashing into the wall and railing. It was as if Emma wielded an invisible force field, effortlessly deflecting anyone who tried to approach her. The more they rushed at her, the more violently they were flung away as if she commanded an unstoppable power of protection.

Emma moved with determination, pushing her way through the crowd of yellow-eyed people until she was directly beneath us. Looking up, she called out a word, "Causidol." Suddenly, a swirling green mist expanded around her, creating a mini tornado that repelled the yellow-eyed people away. Without hesitation, she urged us to join her, "Liam, Sophia, climb down here and stand next to me." As we made our way down, we observed the people attempting to rush us, only to be forcefully repelled by the green mist.

Sophia descended first and rushed over to Emma, enveloping her in a heartfelt hug. As I touched the ground, I stood in awe of the scene unfolding around me. Emma released Sophia from her embrace and turned to smile at me. Returning her smile, I remarked, "So you've learned a new trick."

The soothing warmth of my best friend's embrace was an unexpected comfort after the turmoil that Liam and I had just endured. Emma's composed expression held a sense of relief as she and Liam shared a conversation, but my mind was preoccupied with finding a way out of our current predicament. How long would Emma's enchanting green mist hold the danger at bay? "Emma, I have so many questions for you, but right now, how do we make our escape?" I inquired, scanning our surroundings. Emma directed us to head for the stairs and exit through the front door. She cautioned that the library was no longer safe and promised to explain everything later. Trusting her judgment, I suggested that we should move quickly. Liam silently concurred. As a group, we cautiously advanced towards the stairs, hoping they were still sturdy and would lead us to safety.

We hurried past the yellow-eyed figures, who were getting knocked aside by the power of the eerie green mist. As we reached the staircase, we noticed that the stairs going up to the third floor were in shambles, while the ones leading down to the first floor were unscathed. Despite the yellow-eyed figures attempting to obstruct our way, the green mist effortlessly repelled them, allowing us to continue our journey.

We stepped onto the first floor, and it was a sight of utter devastation. Toppled bookcases, shattered figurines, and broken glass lay strewn across the floor. With Emma leading the way, Liam and I followed, carefully navigating the chaos as we made our way towards the front door. Despite the green mist keeping the figures at bay, they continued to make desperate attempts to reach us. As we approached the entrance, peering through the shattered glass windows, the waiting area appeared eerily empty, providing us with a brief moment of respite to gather our thoughts. Suddenly, a deafening noise from above startled us. Liam's frantic shout urged us to seek cover, and we quickly scrambled under a nearby librarian's desk. Just as we found refuge, glass and metal rained down around us, and I instinctively shut my eyes to shield them from harm.

As the shards of glass ceased falling, I cautiously opened my eyes and found Liam scanning the area for signs of safety. He reassured me that it seemed safe to move. Liam exited the area first, followed by Emma. I emerged from beneath the table and observed them both gazing at the ceiling with wide eyes and open mouths. I followed their gaze and felt my heart sink.

As I looked up, I noticed that the area where the Library skylight used to be was now occupied by the enormous mouth of a dog. Its jaws were moving, with a forked tongue swinging wildly. The dog's teeth were so long that they extended past its jaw and scraped against the ceiling frame. At the same time, I caught a glimpse of a bright light out of the corner of my eye, and when I turned to look, I saw a large yellowed eye with a red hue peering through the side windows of the Library. The eye was so massive that it covered the entire window. As this was happening to my right, I noticed the same phenomenon occurring to my left – a large yellow eye scanning the room, seemingly searching for us.

"We have to move," Liam whispered urgently. Emma and I nodded in agreement and hurried toward the waiting room. Liam reached the door first, only to discover that it was locked. "We have to break the glass," Emma urged. Without hesitation, she sprinted forward and leaped through the window. Liam followed suit, and I did the same, propelled by a sense of urgency.

As we entered the room, we were confronted by more figures with eerie yellow eyes. In a moment of desperation, Emma called upon Causidol using its name, and a green mist engulfed the room, accompanied by a loud popping sound. The mist forcefully expelled everyone onto the street, leaving us gasping for breath as we struggled to regain our composure.

"We can't stay here. Where do we go now?" I panted, feeling the weight of urgency pressing down on us. Emma, after taking a deep breath, stood resolutely and declared, "We'll head to my house. It's nearby, and it should be empty." Liam and I nodded in agreement, giving our silent approval.

As Emma walked toward the front door, Causidol materialized in her paper form, blocking our path.

"Causidol, get out of the way. We have to go," I said. Liam and Sophia were behind me, curious about what was going on.

"If you choose to walk out those doors, you will be stepping out of the void I have created, and Cerberus will track you down. Do you really want to face Cerberus outside, or would you rather stay and confront it here and now?"

"What is this void you're talking about?" Liam asked, next talking about figures with yellow eyes. "They said you hid us in a void - what were they talking about?" Sophia, taking a step forward, pressed, "Causidol, what haven't you been telling us? You told us Cerberus was asleep, and we had two hours. But now it looks like Cerberus is wide awake and right above us. Care to explain?" Their questions resonated deeply with me, but for now, our priority was getting out of there.

"Look, we don't have time for this. We have to keep moving. Causidol, can you keep the green mist going, or when we leave, will that go away?" Causidol assured us that the mist would continue to surround and protect us. "Ok, good. Can the mist cover my house and keep Cerberus away for even a little while?" Causidol nodded and confirmed that it could. "Fine. We are heading to my house to come up with a plan. But Causidol, we're not done. You're going to tell us the truth before we do anything else." Despite Causidol's unchanged expression, she began to turn to mist again and enveloped us. I exchanged a determined look with Sophia and Liam before urging them to keep moving.

With Liam and Sophia right behind me, I summoned all my courage and slowly pushed the creaking front door open. The world outside looked like a scene from a nightmare. Bodies lay inert in the street, but I knew they would soon stir back to life. Gesturing urgently to Liam and Sophia, I signaled that we needed to make a run for it. "We have to get to my house through the park. It's just on the other side, and I'm hoping the Causidol green mist will give us some cover," I whispered urgently.

After a quick check to ensure everyone was ready, I mustered all my resolve and burst through the front door, sprinting across the street toward the park entrance. Sophia followed closely behind me while Liam brought up the rear. We weaved between the wreckage of crashed cars, being careful not to tread on anyone as we made our way to the park.

Reaching the park entrance first, I stole a quick glance behind me to check on the others, only to catch sight of the ominous threat closing in on us.

Through the billowing smoke from the burning trees and the dark clouds above, a large black dog's silhouette emerged, its towering figure casting an ominous shadow over the building. One of its heads was buried in the library's roof, while the others loomed around the structure, peering through the windows with piercing yellow eyes that resembled searchlights. The details of the creature were shrouded in mystery, but one thing was clear — its massive paw, the size of a semi-truck, rested ominously on the ground. The paw was covered in fur as black as the night, and its sharp black claws gouged into the pavement. I felt a sense of urgency to leave the scene behind, urging Sophia and Liam to hasten their pace as we ventured into the park.

The green mist of Causidol seemed to conceal our movements as we cautiously navigated through the once-serene park. This used to be one of my favorite places to visit, but now it is barely recognizable. Scorch marks marred the grass, lifeless flowers littered the ground, trees were ablaze, and the park was strewn with people. Men, women, and children alike, no one was safe from the terror of Cerberus.

We arrived at the playground, where the cheerful sound of children's laughter had filled the air before. But now, all that remained was a scene of devastation. The once vibrant playground lay in ruins, with twisted metal jungle gyms, melted slides, and shattered park benches. There was no joy or laughter to be found in this desolate place.

As Sophia placed her hand on my shoulder, a sense of urgency washed over me. "We have to keep moving before Cerberus notices us," she said calmly. I stole one last glance at the abandoned playground before we hurried on. As we ran, the grand statue of Athena came into view. My admiration for it was mixed with a newfound curiosity about the truths of our world. I silently asked for guidance as we passed the statue, hoping for some semblance of wisdom to guide us. The once lively pound now lay desolate, devoid of the animals that had once inhabited it. It was disheartening to witness the decay of a place I once cherished. Yet, as we pressed forward, the sight only reinforced the gravity of our situation. Cerberus was merely a harbinger of the impending chaos. If his master were able to cross into the realm of the living, I realized that the world would never again know joy.

As we reached the far end of the park, the entrance was visible just ahead. Soon, we would reach my house and have a brief moment of clarity before devising a plan to seal Cerberus away. I still needed to figure out what to sacrifice. I refused to entertain Causidol's suggestion of sacrificing one of my friends. There had to be an alternative solution.

Liam whispered, "Look, I can see Emma's house. We're almost there." He led the way as Sophia and I followed. My attention had wandered back to the park, but now I saw my house in the distance, offering a momentary relief. However, it was short-lived. In the far-off distance behind us, the haunting howl of three wolves echoed through the park. As I turned to look, I saw three sets of glowing yellow eyes floating high above in the sky, obscured by smoke and clouds. The eyes peered straight at us, and I stopped in my tracks. The footsteps of Liam and Sophia were nowhere to be heard. It felt as though the eyes of Cerberus were burning into the depths of my soul. A nameless fear enveloped me, leaving me with a sense of hopelessness.

Beads of sweat trickled down my brow as I stood frozen in terror.

"Emma, you must keep moving. Cerberus has not noticed you; my mist is still shielding you. Don't look into its eyes, as they bring fear from the deepest corners of your soul. Take your friends and follow the plan. Return to your house and be prepared for what happens next."

The haunting melody of Causidol's voice echoed in my mind, jolting me awake from the grip of whatever darkness Cerberus had plunged me into. My eyes fell upon Liam and Sophia, both paralyzed with fear, and I gently rested my hands on their quivering shoulders. The touch seemed to break the spell that had ensnared them. With determination in my voice, I urged them to press on.

We hurried out of the park and dashed across the street. I sprinted up the steps to my porch and grabbed my house keys. After unlocking the door, I swung it open wide and gestured for Liam and Sophia to run inside. They swiftly followed my lead. As they darted inside, I glanced back and silently pleaded with Causidol to conceal us. The green mist that had enveloped us now began to encircle my house. It formed a hazy barrier, offering only a faint glimpse of the outside world. Just before I shut the door, I caught sight of a colossal dark figure moving through the park in the swirling mist. Its massive form loomed above the trees, and three indistinct shapes resembling heads hung low to the ground as if they were searching for our scent. As I closed the door, a pair of piercing yellow eyes met mine from within the mist.

CHAPTER 6
WHAT HAVE I DONE

The room plunged into complete darkness. I was engulfed in an eerie silence, unable to see, hear, or feel anything. It was as though I had been transported to a void, detached from the world of the living. Suddenly, a faint glimmer of light pierced the darkness, gradually illuminating the room. Gasping for air, I collapsed to my knees, relieved to be able to breathe again. Liam and Sophia were also struggling to regain their breath as they lay on the ground. "What just happened?" Liam shouted. Using the table for support, I tried to stand up, still dazed by the experience. Liam asked the same question that was racing through my mind—what was that? Could it be possible that the dog in the book had actually turned its head towards me?

Sophia and Liam both struggled to their feet. Just as Sophia was about to speak, a low, menacing growl cut through the air, freezing us in place. The sound seemed to come from behind us, and a chill ran down my spine. My knees wobbled with fear, and I couldn't bring myself to turn around. Glancing to my left, I saw beads of sweat glistening on Sophia's face, mirroring the terror I felt. On the right, Liam's eyes were wide with an unfamiliar dread. I reached out and clasped their hands tightly. We needed to confront whatever was behind us, even if it meant facing our worst nightmares. Hoping against hope that it was all just a terrible dream, I nodded to Sophia and Liam to show that we were in this together. They both reciprocated the gesture, and we all turned around to confront the source of the growl, only to be met with a sight that left me utterly incredulous.

Before us stood a magnificent and fearsome creature: a towering, three-headed canine. This enormous beast bore a striking resemblance to the legendary three-headed dog from the ancient tales. Its piercing yellow eyes were tinged with a menacing red hue, and atop each head sat powerful horns reminiscent of a mighty goat. The creature's jagged, glowing fangs added to its aura of dread, and its shaggy, matted black fur billowed and danced in the wind like licking flames. Each of its heads was a mirror image of the other, and all three were sharply focused on our presence. Despite its daunting appearance, the creature approached us with a deliberate and unwavering gait, lifting its multiple heads as if measuring its prey.

As the menacing dog advanced, Liam positioned himself protectively between me and Sophia and the terrifying three-headed creature. Liam locked eyes with the middle head of the beast, displaying an unyielding resolve. Despite our shock at his quick reaction, Sophia reached out and grasped his arm for support. The beast raised its heads even higher, baring its formidable fangs, signaling its readiness to attack. We were left paralyzed, realizing that we were powerless to prevent the impending onslaught.

As we stood frozen in fear, we suddenly heard the faint sound of pages flipping behind us. Sophia and I turned around, but Liam remained fixated on the monstrous three-headed dog. We watched in awe as the pages from the book tore themselves out and began swirling above us. The pages then coalesced into a spectral hand, which turned its palm towards the menacing beast. A brilliant green light emanated from the hand, nearly blinding us as it shot forth and struck the three-headed dog, hurling it against the door with tremendous force and splintering the wood as the creature crashed through. In stunned silence, we beheld the dog rising to its feet, its middle head fixing a malevolent gaze upon me as if it were about to pounce. Before anything more could happen, a voice cried out, "What is that thing?" The creature turned its attention towards the source of the voice and lunged, causing chaos and panic as it charged through the room, knocking over bookcases and flipping tables. After the chaotic uproar subsided, an eerie stillness enveloped us, causing a sense of unease as we dreaded the potential return of the menacing three-headed dogs.

Liam's voice echoed through the room, filled with disbelief. "What just happened!" he yelled out. "Emma, Sophia, are you guys..." His words trailed off as his gaze shifted to something behind us. I turned around with the others, and we all watched in astonishment as the remaining pages of the book began to merge, forming the shape of a woman. The swirling pages coalesced until a lady, constructed entirely from paper and covered in incomprehensible writing, stood before us on the table.

As she opened her paper eyelids, a bright green light emanated from her eyes, making it almost impossible to look directly at her. A green mist poured from her paper mouth, enveloping the room in an eerie glow.

I moved closer and inquired, "What or who are you?" The paper lady's head tilted downward, and she gracefully descended from the table. We instinctively took a step back as the towering paper lady now loomed before us. Her height was so great that my head only reached her waist. With piercing green eyes fixed on me, she opened her mouth and began to speak.

"I am the sprite of Causidol, a humble servant of the great mage Merlin and the keeper of the Book of Cerberus. My duty is to watch over those who will undertake the formidable task of sealing Cerberus back into his prison before he raises the Gates of Hades. Emma Harris, time is of the essence. We must hurry before your world is lost."

All of us were stunned into silence. After a long pause, Liam finally spoke up. "Wait, did you just say Cerberus? What are the gates of Hades? How do you even know Emma's name?"

Causidol shifted her body deliberately, fixing her intense gaze on Liam. With cautious precision, she took a measured step towards him, but he remained resolute, refusing to back down. It was a strange sight to witness Liam, typically so reserved, confronting Causidol with an uncharacteristic air of defiance. As for Sophia, her silence spoke volumes, and I couldn't help but wonder at the source of Liam's unwavering determination.

Causidol parted her lips, and an eerie green mist began to curl and billow from her mouth, creating an otherworldly atmosphere. The suspense was palpable as she began to utter mysterious words, and it felt as though the very air around us crackled with an unsettling energy.

"Liam Parker, I already told you my identity; there's no need for repetition. However, I'll clarify. I am the guardian of the

Book of Cerberus, the containment for Cerberus, the fearsome three-headed dog that stands watch at the Gates of Hades. My master, Merlin, entrusted me with the task of safeguarding this book. If the day ever comes when Cerberus is set free from his prison, it is my duty to aid whoever possesses the potential to reseal Cerberus and prevent him from opening the Gates to bring about the end of the world."

Sophia, with a hint of fear still lingering in her eyes, finally found the courage to address the sprite. "You still didn't answer his one question, and I have more. But first, answer this: how do you know Liam and Emma's names?" Causidol slowly turned her head towards Sophia and began to speak.

"Dear Sophia Cook, I am the guardian of the Book of Cerberus. My spirit is intertwined with the book, allowing me to perceive all that occurs in its vicinity. I witnessed Emma succumb to Cerberus' enchantment and deliver the book to you. As you opened the Book of Cerberus, I watched as everyone began to lose their vitality. I also saw Emma chant "emittere" and release Cerberus from his confinement. I have complete knowledge and insight into all events involving the Book of Cerberus."

"Wait, did you just say that I unleashed Cerberus?" I exclaimed, stunned. Causidol met my gaze with her mesmerizing glowing green eyes and nodded in affirmation. "But how is that even possible? All I did was utter the word 'release' in Latin," I asked, bewildered.

"Many people may consider Latin a dead language, but it is not truly dead, just forgotten. During my time, Latin was used in spell casting. It's a powerful language, and each word holds significant power. Only those with a strong connection to magic can effectively use Latin to cast spells. However, fragments of Merlin and Cerberus's magic still lingered within the book. All it took was for someone to speak the words for the spell to take effect. Cerberus could sense your understanding of Latin and used his influence to persuade you to take the book. He manipulated you into carrying out his bidding, and now he is free. Emma Harris, you should not blame yourself; you had no control over the outcome."

"That's easy for you to say. Now, because of me, Cerberus is loose and just destroyed the Library! I haven't heard anything out-side this room. Hey, all-knowing book, did you know that there are kids downstairs? What happened to them?" I put my face in my hands, asking myself what I had done, and began to cry.

Sophia wrapped her arms around me, offering comfort and reassurance. She in-sisted that it wasn't my fault and that I shouldn't blame myself, but her words did little to ease my distress. Liam, consumed by anger, confronted Causidol, demand-ing to know why he didn't intervene to prevent Cerberus from manipulating me into setting him free.

"From the wear and tear evident on my pages, it's clear that my magical abilities have waned over time. I was only able to prevent Cerberus from claiming your souls

and push him away from you when he was about to strike. At present, my capabilities are limited to maintaining this form and providing guidance to all of you."

"Wait, what do you mean by 'take our souls'?" I asked. Causidol closed her eyes and began to speak.

"Cerberus sustains himself by consuming souls. After being trapped and neglected for some time, he has weakened considerably. However, as he prowls through the city, he will seek out souls to devour, fueling his recovery and allowing him to grow back to his full size and strength. Once fully revitalized, he will unleash his immense power to dig and raise the gates of Hades, posing a grave threat to all who dwell in the world of the living."

"Okay, that's a lot to process. First of all, I want to express my gratitude for saving us. Secondly, I still believe that there could have been more done to prevent all of this from happening. And lastly, you keep emphasizing that we must stop Cerberus. But, Causidol, did you realize that we are just kids? We've only just graduated from ninth grade. We can't handle this on our own. We need to call our parents and ask for their help if this is all true," Sophia said.

I finally shook off my grief and stood back up. "Yeah, Sophia is right. My dad is the Fire Chief, Sophia's dad is the Police Chief, and her mom is the Mayor. They'll know what to do. Let's call them and let them know what's going on."

I reached for my phone and attempted to call my dad, but to my dismay, I couldn't get a signal. I turned to Sophia to ask if her phone was working, and she shook her head in frustration. Liam also took out his phone and encountered the same issue. I turned to Causidol for an explanation, but she simply pointed her paper finger toward the window. It was then that we realized we had been so engrossed in our library activities that we hadn't noticed the unusual situation outside.

The once bright and sunny sky had transformed into a grim scene filled with swirling dark grey clouds that appeared like a menacing vortex. The city skyline, which I had admired before picking up the book, was now unrecognizable. The once majestic buildings now stood broken and ablaze, casting a ghostly hue against the sky. Trees added to the desolation as they were engulfed in flames, painting the sky in shades of grey. Everywhere I looked, houses lay in ruin, evoking the aftermath of a savage tornado. The streets were a chaotic mess, cluttered with twisted and mangled cars as if they had engaged in a violent collision. The most harrowing sight of all was the numerous people strewn on the ground and hanging out of their vehicles, creating a distressing tableau reminiscent of a scene from a horror film.

I asked Causidol, "What's going on?" She slowly opened her eyes, and in an instant, the room was engulfed in blinding light. We found ourselves standing high above our town, witnessing the terrifying spectacle of Cerberus wreaking havoc and leaving destruction in its wake. The setting shifted to the police station, and we peered down as Sophia's father issued urgent commands to his officers. In the midst of his speech, the roof was violently torn away, and we caught a chilling glimpse of the silhouette of a three-headed dog looming over them. The expressions on their faces were etched with profound shock and disbelief.

The scene changed once more, and suddenly we found ourselves at the scene of a house fire. My father was at the forefront, expertly directing his team in battling the fierce blaze. As he commanded his men, a sudden commotion caught our attention from behind. Unable to turn around, we saw the alarmed expressions on the faces of the firefighters as they glimpsed Cerberus approaching.

The setting shifted to City Hall, where we found ourselves in Sophia's mother's office. She was multitasking, answering phones, and giving instructions to her staff. Suddenly, the doors burst open, causing everyone to fall to the ground. We couldn't turn around, but we could hear Cerberus growling as the employees in Liam's mother's office began to scream.

The setting changes to a rectangular blue building surrounded by parked cars. The building is adorned with windows wrapping around it, allowing visibility from all angles. As we approached, we found ourselves peering through the window and catching a glimpse of Liam's sister, Charlotte, and an older dark-skinned woman with a striking afro. Both were dressed in blue and wore aprons with the words "Bluebird Cafe." It became clear that this was Liam's mother's cafe. Liam frantically screamed, trying to warn his family, but they couldn't hear him. Suddenly, all the windows shattered, showering the area with glass. The last thing we witnessed was Cerberus entering the cafe, causing panic and screams from within. The vision ended, and we found ourselves back in the clubroom, deeply disturbed by what we had just seen and grappled with unspoken questions.

"The scene I just shared with you depicts the devastation caused by Cerberus. While I didn't show you the complete extent of the damage to your family, witnessing the aftermath should make it clear why it's cru-

cial to imprison Cerberus. It's not a matter of being deserving, but rather, you are the sole survivors tasked with this vital responsibility."

We're all still grappling with the shocking events we just witnessed. The sense of loss and confusion is overwhelming. Are our parents truly gone? Is it just us left in town? It feels surreal, like a nightmare we can't wake up from. I started the day like any other, getting ready for the last day of school, but it spiraled into chaos when I accidentally unleashed a terrifying creature on our town, resulting in everyone disappearing. Sophia urgently grabbed my arm, her tears flowing uncontrollably as she struggled to stay on her feet. Liam rushed to her side, gently helping her sit down as she gasped for air between sobs.

My mind was racing, desperately searching for a solution. It fell on us to confront Cerberus and put an end to the mayhem. "Causidol, can we still save our parents, or are they truly gone?" I implored, my heart heavy with fear. Despite her paper form, her sorrowful expression conveyed all the emotions of a living being on the brink of tears.

"The souls of your parents and the other townspeople are not lost, but they are trapped. Cerberus has been absorbing these souls and storing them within his body. If you can manage to seal him, the souls will be released and returned to their rightful owners. However, you must seal Cerberus before he is able to open the Gates of Hades. If you are unsuccessful, the souls will be lost forever."

After hearing that, Liam stood back up, determination in his eyes. "So there's still a chance we can save everyone?" Liam asked, looking at Causidol for confirmation. She nodded solemnly, indicating that there was hope. "What do we need to do, Causidol?" Liam asked, eager to take action. Meanwhile, Sophia managed to compose herself and stood next to Liam. "No, Liam, we can't. It's too dangerous. There has to be someone else who can do this," Sophia said, holding his hand tightly. Liam locked eyes with Sophia and said, "I will save your parents, Emma's dad, my family, and everyone else in town." The sudden display of bravery from Liam was surprising, as he had never shown this side of himself before. "Liam, where is all this coming from? You've never been this outgoing before,"

Emma asked, curious about this sudden change. Liam looked down, closed his eyes, and said, "I lost my dad, and that's a pain I could never get over. I don't want Sophia to go through the same pain we've been through, Emma. No one is going to lose a loved one today, don't you agree?" Hearing Liam's words, I realized that I never wanted anyone else to feel the pain of losing a loved one. "You're right, Liam. We need to do this," she said, feeling resolute. "Are you both crazy? We are only kids. This is way above our heads. We will get hurt or worse, end up like our parents!" Sophia started screaming, tears flowing down her cheeks. I moved closer to her and said, "Remember when you said you wished you could go on an adventure and make history like the people you read about? Well, now here's your chance. You won't just be making history, but you will be saving your parents. Don't get me wrong, I'm terrified. I don't want to do this either. But you saw what I saw; we are the only ones left. If you don't want to come, that's okay. It really should be me since this is my fault. Liam, you can stay with Sophia and keep her safe."

Sophia's eyes widened in a mix of fear and determination as she spoke with a hint of anger in her voice. "There is no way I'm letting you do this alone. I'm honestly too scared to move, but you and Liam are my only friends, and I can't live with myself if something happens to you. It's against my better judgment, but let's do this." Liam echoed the same sentiment. I couldn't ask for better friends. I turned my attention toward Causidol and said, "Alright, once again, what do we need to do?"

Chapter 7
Dark Ages

Now that we were all in consensus that we had the responsibility of saving everyone, we knew we had to come up with a plan. "Causidol, can you tell us about Cerberus' current location and how much time we have before he begins to dig?" I inquired. Causidol's eye emitted a luminous green glow as she slowly levitated off the ground. As she spoke, her mouth opened, and an eerie green mist began to emanate from it.

"Cerberus has come to a stop and settled down in a quiet corner of the park. Despite

appearing to have regained full strength, he is taking a moment to rest before beginning to dig. This respite is to be expected, as summoning the Gate of Hades will require an enormous amount of energy. He will remain asleep until he senses his body becoming more settled."

"Alright, that's comforting," I mused silently. "Wait, why is he taking a break? Why hasn't he pursued us? Maybe he doesn't perceive us as a threat," Liam pondered aloud.

"Cerberus is completely unaware that you are all still alive. While I may not possess much power, I am still able to do a little. I have skillfully hidden our presence here in the library. You are free to explore the entire library without any apprehension. If Cerberus were to discover your presence here, he would certainly come."

Liam expressed relief at the opportunity to devise a plan without the looming threat of an unexpected intrusion. However, I still had some pressing questions for Causidol. I inquired about the amount of time remaining before Cerberus would reawaken.

"Cerberus is expected to awaken in approximately two hours, at which point his body should be fully prepared to rise the Gates."

We only have a two-hour window to devise a plan to save the world, with the clock ticking fast. Before I could voice my concerns, Sophia took charge. "If I've understood correctly, we have just two hours to figure out a way to contain Cerberus, but we still lack vital information about how and why this all began. I need to understand the history behind why Cerberus was sealed away and how Merlin achieved it. If we have two hours, I'd like to dedicate at least twenty minutes to uncovering what transpired." Sophia couldn't have articulated it any better. It was fitting for the resident historian to delve into the back story. Causidol nodded in agreement and began recounting her narrative.

"In an era more than a hundred thousand years ago, the world teemed with an unfathomable amount of magic and wonder. Gods and mortals coexisted in perfect harmony, and among them, the renowned mage Merlin was honing his extraordinary skills, earning widespread acclaim throughout the land. Each deity presided over their

respective domain, but one god harbored resentment and aspirations for greater power. Hades, the embittered ruler of the underworld and sovereign of the deceased, yearned for supremacy in the divine hierarchy.

At the solstice, when all the gods would convene, Hades, the ruler of the underworld, longed to claim the throne from his brother and emerge as the sole deity governing mortals. Being bound to his kingdom, he could not amass forces to overthrow his brother and seize the throne. Hence, he devised a plan, deciding to bestow half of his considerable power upon his most trusty companion, Cerberus.

At the next Winter Solstice, Hades planned to bring Cerberus from the underworld to the world of the living. During the *meeting of the Gods on Mount Olympus, Cerberus would use his immense power to unearth and construct a new gate, connecting our world to the underworld. As the Gods assembled on Olympus, Cerberus diligently dug and ultimately created what we now know as the Gates of Hades. Upon completion, Cerberus opened the gates, releasing the full force of the underworld onto the living.*

In the tumultuous Chaso region and beyond, a great conflict raged on between the forces of the Gods and the dark powers. For years, battles between the Gods and other Mages against these dark forces had ensued, with an ominous tilt in favor of Hades. This was all made possible by the influence of Cerberus. With the Gates of Hades open, the underworld unleashed chaos that bol-

stered Hades's strength, surpassing that of the other gods. This era, though its name has evolved over time, is remembered as the Dark Ages.

One fateful day, Zeus, the powerful lord of the sky, and his esteemed general Athena sought the counsel of the legendary wizard Merlin. Desperate to bring an end to the ongoing war and restore peace to the world, they implored Merlin for his aid. In response, Merlin proposed a daring plan. Rather than directly confronting Hades, their true challenge lay in neutralizing Cerberus, the guardian responsible for keeping the gates open. Once Cerberus was contained, the divine beings could then seal the gate, stripping Hades of his dominion. To achieve this, Merlin conceived a formidable prison to confine Cerberus and suppress his *influence. It had to be impregnable, ensuring that Cerberus could never break free. Ultimately, Merlin decided to bind Cerberus within the pages of a book, condemning him to eternal captivity.*

Merlin dedicated many years to meticulously inscribing spells, crafting incantations, and etching runes into a book in order to imprison Cerberus. He also designed me to serve as the guardian of the prison, responsible for ensuring that Cerberus remained under control. Once the book was completed and the world faced imminent peril, the remaining gods and Mages united for a final assault. Athena devised a strategy for everyone to stage a coordinated attack on Hades, luring him and his forces away while leaving Cerberus unguarded.

As the epic battle raged on between the formidable Hades and the mighty Zeus, the legendary sorcerer Merlin advanced toward the towering Gates guarded by the fearsome Cerberus. The three-headed guardian exuded an aura of terror that sent shivers down the spine and conjured the darkest fears lurking in the recesses of one's mind. Undaunted, Merlin steeled himself against the overwhelming dread and summoned his courage. With an incantation, he unleashed a powerful spell, ensnaring Cerberus within the enchanting pages of the legendary Book of Cerberus before the monstrous guardian could retaliate. Another mystical incantation sealed the gates shut. At that moment, Hades found himself stripped of his formidable powers and rendered utterly powerless.

The Dark Ages had come to an end, and the world was changing. Merlin had emerged as the savior of the realm. His renown spread far and wide, and he made the decision to safeguard the Book of Cerberus, believing only in his own ability to protect it. However, as years passed and generations aged, Merlin himself began to feel the weight of time. In an era of transition, as ancient deities faded away and new powers rose, the tale of the Dark Ages was consigned to history, giving birth to something entirely different.

As for the ancient tome, I embarked on a worldwide journey, traversing countless libraries in a ceaseless effort to keep the formidable Cerberus power contained within its fading pages. Despite my best efforts, the mystical wards that had restrained Cer-

berus were gradually waning. I utilized my limited sway to persuade mortal beings to transport us to this secluded library location tucked away in a distant corner where we would remain undisturbed.

As my powers diminished to the point where even Cerberus could sense you, Emma, I hadn't anticipated your presence. Despite my attempts to guide you away, his strength surpassed mine at that moment. That's how it all transpired, leading to my current state. I hope you now comprehend that Cerberus is merely a tool for ushering in a new era of darkness. If he manages to raise the gate and unlock the doors to the underworld, it won't just be monsters emerging. Hades himself will return to complete what he initiated."

I stared in disbelief at Causidol, a figure with a body made of paper and emitting a green mist. Her story seemed preposterous, yet the fate of the world now rested on our shoulders. We were tasked with sealing Cerberus so that Hades could be confined and unable to wreak havoc on the earth. This certainly wasn't how I expected to kick off my summer.

As the weight of the situation settled in, I interjected, "If that's the whole story, we have a major problem." Liam, seemingly oblivious to the gravity of the situation, retorted, "What do you mean? Causidol just laid out the plan: confront Cerberus, recite a spell, and trap him back in the book. We'll be the heroes." I shook my head and argued, "It's not that simple. Causidol mentioned her pages have faded, meaning she doesn't have the magic to contain Cerberus anymore." Liam's expression shifted as the realization dawned on him.

"Is there really no other option?" Liam suggested, frustration evident in his voice. Sophia shook her head, "We can't afford to spend years rewriting the book like Merlin did. We have only two hours." It was true; time was not on our side. I chimed in, "And even if we had the time, we don't possess the same otherworldly abilities that Merlin had." Liam furrowed his brow in deep thought, clearly searching for a solution. We were all feeling the pressure as the clock kept ticking. Turning to Causidol, I pleaded, "Is there any other way we can seal Cerberus?" Causidol closed her eyes, deep in contemplation.

"To effectively contain Cerberus, a powerful spell can be spoken to bind Cerberus to an item using specific words imbued with fear. The chosen item, such as a book, can then be used as a secure vessel to confine Cerberus. The pages of the book act as layers that can effectively compress Cerberus's power, serving as a formidable prison to contain its strength. The potency of the spell and the fear embedded within the words will dictate the strength of the confinement. Although items can also be used for binding, it is recommended to utilize a book for this task due to its efficacy."

"Ok, that's a good start, thanks Causidol," I said, turning to Liam and Sophia. "If I understand correctly, we need items that Cerberus would fear. I'm not sure what that would be, but I believe if we put our heads together, we can figure something out." Liam nodded in agreement while Sophia had her hand over her mouth, lost in thought. I asked her what she was pondering. "I think we still need a book because if it's true that the pages of a book can hold Cerberus back, it makes sense to use a book now," Sophia said. I reminded her that we don't have time to write a book, to which she responded, "What if the book was already written?"

Liam and I exchanged puzzled glances in response to Sophia's enigmatic statement. "What book could possibly have what we need already?" Liam queried. "Consider this: what book would be so formidable that it could instill fear in every monster because of its sheer power?" Sophia asked. Despite her question, Liam and I remained bewildered. Sophia sighed and said, "The Bible."

Sophia was right about the Bible's powerful scriptures being capable of keeping Cerberus at bay, which left Liam impressed. "Sophia, you're a genius!" he exclaimed, causing Sophia's cheeks to flush with embarrassment at the compliment. "There's a religious section in the history department. I remember seeing an Old Testament Bible in a display case. I think it might still be there," Sophia suggested. This news brought a glimmer of hope, but there was uncertainty lingering in the air. Seeking reassurance, I turned to Causidol and asked, "Would the Bible really be enough?"

"In theory, the Bible has the potential to seal Cerberus, but it's not its primary fo-

cus. While the Bible is powerful, its main purpose isn't specifically to seal Cerberus. To effectively contain Cerberus, you will need to combine the power of the Bible with another external item. By using the Bible along with another item, you can strengthen the containment of Cerberus and prevent its escape."

"Okay, so we still need something else, but we don't know what. Anyone got any ideas?" I asked, feeling a bit puzzled. Liam hesitantly raised his hand. "I know this might sound silly, but in the monster movies that I've watched, they always use specific items to hurt or ward off monsters. Maybe there's something in the film section that could give us some insight," Liam suggested. "No, that's not silly at all. It actually could be really helpful. In those movies, they used wooden stakes for vampires and silver for werewolves. There might be something else that could work, something we're not thinking about right now," I responded, nodding in agreement. Sophia had a proud look on her face as she glanced over at Liam. He met her gaze and started to look a bit embarrassed. "Okay, guys, it looks like we've got a book to find and some more research to do," I said, but just as I finished speaking, Causidol interjected.

"All of this is great, but you still need an incantation. A spell that can activate the items and form a new prison. Merlin was very careful in how he spoke to make sure Cerberus was bound by the book. I agree with your plan so far, but everything must be in order before we confront Cerberus. I

*suggest Emma stays with me, and we for-
mulate a spell that will work. Since Emma
is the only one of you who can speak Latin,
she needs to be the one who casts the spell."*

I stood my ground, "Sorry, Causidol,
but I'm not comfortable with the idea
of splitting up." Sophia placed her hands
on my shoulders, her eyes filled with urgency as she insisted, "We don't have time.
We have to split up. I'll go downstairs
to retrieve the Bible I saw, and Liam can
check out the film section for anything
that might help us." Liam chimed in, men-
tioning that the library was shielded, so we
didn't have to worry about Cerberus chas-
ing after us. Despite my unease, I had to
acknowledge their points; time was of the
essence, and we needed to keep moving.

Despite my reservations, I knew we had no other option. I declared, "Let's make a pact to regroup in this room before we do anything else." Both Sophia and Liam nodded in solemn agreement. I embraced Sophia and exchanged a fist bump with Liam, reminding them to exercise caution. As they headed towards the door, they cautiously peeked out to assess the surroundings. Liam signaled his approval with a thumbs-up before they departed, leaving Causidol and me alone in the room.

After Liam and I left the clubroom, I expected it to be a quick dash to the second floor to retrieve the Bible I had spotted. However, nothing could have prepared me for what awaited us there. The third floor of the library was in shambles. Office doors lay scattered and blown off, with glass strewn all over the place. The chaos continued as bookshelves lay toppled, and books were scattered in all directions. It was as if a tornado had ripped through the area, leaving behind a scene of utter devastation. But the most chilling sight was yet to come. Those who had remained on the third floor were strewn across the ground, unmoving. Their pallid skin and distant, unfocused gazes filled me with a sense of dread. I approached a young boy perched against the wall, looking like he belonged in middle school, donning a matching Power Rangers shirt and hat. As I reached out to touch him, his icy cold skin sent shivers down my spine.

I attempted to communicate with him, but all I received in response was a hollow, yawning sound, his vacant eyes refusing to meet mine. It was as though the life within him had vanished, leaving behind an empty vessel.

Liam, who was behind me, urgently gestured for us to keep moving. It was incredibly difficult to focus on the mission at hand, knowing that my mom was likely in the same perilous situation. I pushed the distracting thoughts aside - there was no time to dwell on personal worries. The fate of our families hung in the balance, and failure was not an option.

As we carefully navigated the chaotic scene, stepping over sprawled bodies, the gravity of the situation weighed heavily on us. The sheer number of people in need of help made our progress slow and difficult. Finally reaching the stairs, we were met with a disheartening sight - the staircase had collapsed, blocking our path to the second floor.

"The damage caused by Cerberus is unbelievable. It feels like we were only in that room for a few minutes," Liam remarked, voicing the shock we both felt. "Perhaps the Causidol's magic shielded us so well that time seemed to slip away," I mused in response. Liam nodded in agreement and scanned the area, searching for an alternative route to the second floor.

"You know, the elevators are right over there. Maybe we could give them a try," Liam suggested. I agreed - at this point, it was worth a shot.

We made our way to the elevator, and Liam confidently pressed the button to summon it. To our surprise, the elevator sprang to life and began ascending. "Finally, some progress," I thought to myself. As the elevator came to a stop and the doors slid open with a gentle ding, my heart sank. A group of small children huddled in the corner, with the same pale skin and eerie, lifeless eyes as the boy we had just encountered. There were around fifteen of them, clinging to each other with looks of unmistakable fear etched across their faces.

Tears welled up in my eyes and began to trickle down my face. The heart-wrenching sight of these helpless kids overwhelmed me, causing me to crumple to the ground, my knees unable to support me any longer. Liam rushed to my side, comforting me with gentle strokes on my back and reassurances that everything would be alright. But at that moment, nothing felt okay. Cerberus, the three-headed dog, had snatched away the innocent souls of these children and was now nowhere to be found, off-napping somewhere. These kids should be concerned about eating their vegetables, not about being pursued by a menacing mythical creature.

"Their parents must have placed them in the elevator, believing that Cerberus wouldn't be able to reach them," Liam said. I stood up, wiped my face, and declared, "Cerberus will regret this. You were right; we are going to rescue everyone."

Liam raised his fist triumphantly and let out a cheer. I couldn't fully comprehend the agony that he and Emma experienced after losing one of their parents. However, witnessing the heinous act of someone targeting children ignited an intense reaction within me. Despite not having a strong connection with young children, a profound sense of justice surged through me. The sight of these innocent kids enduring such turmoil filled me with both sadness and overwhelming anger. Recalling my father's belief that it was the responsibility of adults to safeguard the younger generation and my mother's view that every child in town was like her own, I wondered if I was channeling my father's and mother's emotions. If so, I resolved to harness that connection as a driving force to persevere.

Liam and I entered the elevator, attempting to block out the presence of the children behind us. Once inside, Liam pressed the button for the second floor, and the door was sealed shut. The flickering lights threatened to stir up fear within me, but I felt a sudden warmth as Liam took hold of my hand. It was unclear whether he did it to reassure me or to find solace himself, but either way, I was grateful for his comforting gesture.

As the elevator came to a halt and the doors chimed open, we both exited and were greeted by the same chaotic scene that we had encountered on the third floor. Bookcases lay toppled over, windows shattered, and a fire had ignited in the corner near the librarian's desk, though it didn't seem to pose an immediate threat. I couldn't help but think that it might extinguish itself. Additionally, there were individuals sprawled out all over the place, in the same lifeless state as the people we had seen upstairs and the children in the elevator.

I peered down the path I needed to take and was met with a blockade of toppled bookcases obstructing my way. As I glanced in Liam's direction, I noticed that the hallway connecting us to the film section was enveloped in darkness, resembling a black hole with the lights completely off.

"Sophia, if you're still struggling, we don't have to split up. I can stay with you," Liam said, his voice filled with concern. His offer was incredibly kind, but I knew that time was of the essence, and we had to split up. "I appreciate that, Liam, but we really don't have time. We need to split up," I said, trying to convey the urgency of the situation. Liam's disappointment was evident, but he nodded in understanding. After wishing each other to be careful, he headed towards the dark hallway. I hope this isn't the last time I see him. I really wanted to go on that cookie date.

Splitting away from Sophia felt like I was abandoning her, but she was right - time was of the essence. As I hurried toward the hallway, the lights suddenly went out, plunging the corridor into darkness. I ventured in cautiously, but before I knew it, I stumbled and fell to the ground, unable to see what had caused me to trip. The eerie sound of a hollow, echoing groan filled the air, sending shivers down my spine. It dawned on me that there were likely other people scattered throughout the hallway, just like the lifeless figures we had encountered earlier.

I stood up and cautiously made my way down the hall, taking care not to bump into anyone. As I reached the end of the hallway, where the film room was located, I found that the lights were still on, providing a semblance of comfort. However, what awaited me inside the room was anything but reassuring. The space was in shambles. The screens lay shattered, and the furniture was upturned and broken into pieces. The glass display cases were all smashed, and the once cherished memorabilia lay strewn across the floor, now in pieces. Books were scattered everywhere, their pages torn out and ripped to shreds.

My hope of finding a helpful book in this chaos had been dashed.

I found myself muttering, "Come on, Liam, there has to be something I can find," as I rummaged through the wreckage, but my efforts turned up nothing. Realizing I couldn't afford to spend any more time there, I knew I had to find Sophia. Perhaps she would have an idea of what we could do. Exiting the film room, I felt defeated as I cautiously made my way down the dimly lit hallway, the hollow yawns of lifeless bodies echoing around me. Finally, reaching the end of the corridor, I caught sight of the elevator where Sophia and I had gone our separate ways.

I walked over to the elevator and stood there, consumed by a wave of self-doubt. "All that bravado, and yet here I am with nothing to show for it. How can I face Emma and Sophia empty-handed?" I muttered to myself. Emma was upstairs crafting a spell to banish Cerberus, while Sophia was confronting her fears of retrieving a Bible that would serve as Cerberus's new prison. And here I was, talking a big game but falling short yet again. As I wallowed in embarrassment, the flickering sound of flames drew my attention to the librarian's desk. The fire was growing but was not yet a cause for alarm. My gaze shifted upward, following the flames, and landed on a sign that read "Horror and Gothic Literature This Way."

I made a mad dash towards the desk, my eyes wide with a sudden surge of hope. I frantically followed the arrow pointing to the left, darting between toppled bookcases and overturned carts. Though people still lay strewn across the floor, I couldn't spare them a second glance. The metal poles with bent arrows led me to the horror and gothic section, and with newfound confidence, I pressed on.

As I approached the doorway to the horror and gothic section, a sense of dread washed over me. What I saw inside was even more chilling than what I had encountered in the film room. The tall, imposing bookshelves made of dark wood were haphazardly strewn across the floor, spilling their contents of torn and mangled books. Some of the shelves lay broken and splintered, adding to the chaotic scene with scattered wooden fragments. Even the rare books protected by glass enclosures had not escaped the destruction, their shattered glass mingling with the torn pages and covers. Vintage armchairs lay upturned; small reading tables were overturned, and shattered lamps littered the ground, adding to the sense of disarray. The posters and framed artwork that once adorned the walls now lay in tatters, bearing deep claw marks. Meanwhile, thematic signs and book labels, once neatly displayed, now lay in ruins, torn from their rightful places and scattered across the damaged floor.

As I cautiously made my way through the room, my mind raced with disbelief. It seemed impossible that Cerberus could have caused this much destruction in such a short span of time. I carefully trod across the room, the sound of broken glass crunching beneath my shoes as

I navigated through the debris. My eyes scanned the chaotic scene, searching for any semblance of order. Amidst the torn and tattered books, I desperately sought something, anything, that could provide a clue or a solution. Alas, all I found were useless, shredded pages, and I realized I was as lost and hopeless as before.

I could hardly believe my luck when I stumbled upon it. At first, I thought I was seeing things, but there it was — a book emanating an eerie dark red glow, its cover adorned with the face of an ancient weathered man sporting fangs like a vampire. As I gingerly picked up the book, I saw glass shards tumbling out from within its pages. After carefully removing all the glass, I turned the book over and read the title: "Bound by Shadows: Ancient Methods of

Monster Restraint" by Elias Grimwood. Could it really be this easy? Had I finally found the book I had been searching for?

Eagerly, I flipped through the pages, hoping to find something useful. However, the book was badly damaged, with torn pages and missing sections. Just as I was about to lose hope, I stumbled upon a single intact page. I read the words aloud, "In many cultures, chains—particularly those forged from black iron—were believed to have the power to restrain and weaken malevolent entities. The binding of a demon or monster with such chains not only immobilized the creature but also drained it of its supernatural strength, rendering it harmless. These chains, often consecrated through ancient rituals, symbolized the triumph of order over chaos and good over evil."

As I realized what we were missing, a sense of urgency gripped me. I knew that iron chains would be the key to sealing the book shut, ensuring that no one would ever be able to open it. Time was ticking away, and I had to hurry back to meet up with Sophia. I quickly tucked the book under my arm and sprinted back to the elevator, hoping that Sophia had been successful in her endeavors as well.

As Liam rushed towards the ominous dark hallway, I couldn't help but feel a sense of unease. Despite my worries about his safety, I couldn't deny that he had displayed a remarkable amount of courage recently. It was a stark contrast to the old Liam, who used to show up late and remain lost in thoughts about his future film projects. Even Emma had stepped up, diligently attempting to learn a spell that could fend off Cerberus. The pressure on her to master it was palpable. While I could easily find books and Liam could search for additional information, the responsibility of uttering the correct incantation in Latin still rested solely on Emma's shoulders.

In the clubroom, I felt fearless as I confidently conversed and acted as if fear was nonexistent. However, now I am frozen with fear, regrettably sending Liam away when I should have embraced his company. I convinced myself that I would hinder his progress, but now I realize I need his support more than ever.

The overwhelming grip of fear threatened to paralyze me, but I couldn't bear the thought of letting down my family and friends – my mom, dad, Emma, and Liam. They were all depending on me, and I couldn't afford to succumb to my own terror. Gathering my resolve, I took a deep breath and turned toward the direction where the Regiluos section was located. Despite the obstacles of toppled bookshelves blocking my path, I knew I could surmount them with ease. With determination, I murmured to myself, "It's now or never."

I hurried over to the toppled bookshelves and began to scale them. As I climbed higher, I couldn't help but notice a faint and eerie sound that seemed to grow with each step. Finally reaching the summit, I gazed out over the devastation caused by Cerberus. The library lay in ruins as though a savage beast had torn through it. Deep claw marks marred the walls and tables, bookcases lay shattered, and books were strewn about in tatters.

As I descended, the faint sound intensified, echoing ominously. As I reached the base, it felt as though the sound was right behind me. Peering through the disheveled bookshelves, I spotted people trapped underneath, wearing the same lifeless expressions. They did not move, only hollowly yawning with vacant, glossy gray eyes.

As I took a step back, I suddenly felt my foot make contact with something yielding. I pivoted around and peered down, only to discover another person lying motionless on the ground. Their eyes were fixed on the ceiling as if nothing else in the world existed. The swirling grey clouds in their eyes gave off an aura of profound emptiness, making me feel as though I was gazing into a vortex. Their gaping mouth emitted a hollow yawn that reverberated in the air.

I had to constantly remind myself that the only way to aid them was for me to retrieve the book and confront Cerberus. With a sense of urgency, I increased my speed and began my journey towards the history department. Despite the haunting sound of yawning echoing through the corridors, I fixed my gaze ahead, attempting to block out the scattered cries of distress from the people around me. It was challenging, but I remained focused and persisted in moving forward.

I rushed to the history department with urgency, heading straight for the Religious section. As I arrived, the scene was one of havoc and devastation. Bookcases lay overturned, and books were strewn across the floor. Turning left, I was met with a disarray of the Religious section. Tall wooden bookshelves had been toppled, spilling religious texts onto the ground. Sacred volumes and religious books lay torn, with pages ripped out and covers damaged. Tables and chairs were upended, some with broken legs while reading lamps lay shattered. Precious religious artwork had been torn from the walls, and broken glass frames littered the ground. The display case housing the sought-after book was smashed, and ancient artifacts lay in ruin.

As I made my way through the wreckage, the enormity of the damage weighed heavily on my mind. Amidst the chaos, I found myself searching desperately for an old Bible, a glimmer of hope amidst all the destruction. I carefully scanned the floor, my eyes trained for any sign of what I sought. Then, I stumbled upon a broken picture of Jesus, the frame crushed and the image crumpled. Gently, I picked it up and leaned it against the wall, closing my eyes for a moment as I whispered a silent plea for help. As I opened my eyes and surveyed the scene once more, my gaze fell upon something that caught my attention—a deep brown book with gold lettering and a bold cross on the front. It was massive, standing at about two feet tall and a foot wide. Although the cover was scratched and torn and the pages ripped, some even torn out, it was a precious find amidst the devastation, offering a glimmer of comfort and solace.

As I clutched the worn book to my chest, I marveled at its imperfect state, finding solace in its presence. A picture of Jesus offered me silent reassurance as I expressed my gratitude. Hurrying back to meet Liam, my steps quickened, driven by the desire to reunite with my friends. The eerie echoes of distant howls seemed to propel me forward, urging me on. Reaching the blockade of towering bookshelves, I hoisted myself up, determined to reach the top. With each movement, I clung to the hope that had not yet faded. Finally, as I gazed down from the summit, a wave of despair washed over me, clouding my thoughts.

Chapter 8
Discovered

Liam and Sophia took off, leaving me alone with Causidol, the towering figure made of paper and swirling green smoke. Our mission was clear: we needed to devise an incantation to seal Cerberus away. Despite my unease about splitting up, Sophia was right—we were running out of time. I was grateful that she took charge, even though inside, I was panicking. This whole situation had been beyond chaotic from the beginning. I had inadvertently unleashed a three-headed dog onto the world, and now I had to seal him away before he could plunge the world into chaos by opening a gate to the underworld and freeing Hades from his prison. It was the last thing any teenage girl would want to go through before starting tenth grade.

The moment had come to stop panicking and begin working. I decided to postpone any panic until after I had completed everything. I turned to Causidol and inquired about our starting point. She moved closer to me before starting to speak.

"Emma, do you recall the tale I shared about Merlin and his incredible strength in magic?"

"Sure, I remember the story. It was very fantasy-heavy, not really my style. I understand that it all happened because you're standing in front of me, and I'm still processing the idea that a lady made out of book paper and green mist is the only solution to our problem. If you don't mind, I would like to hurry up and get on with this," I said. Despite having a face constructed of paper, Causidol managed to convey her displeasure at my tone through her expression.

"Emma Harris, I know you're concerned about your loved ones, but I won't tolerate being spoken to in that manner. If this responsibility is overwhelming for you, I'm sorry. I wish someone older and more respectful could take your place. But you're all I have, and I'm committed to fulfilling my duty. Will you cooperate with me?"

As I reflected on the situation, it became clear that she was right; my behavior had been disrespectful. It wasn't intentional, but the urgency of the situation led my friends to scatter through the library in an attempt to rectify the error I had made. While everyone assured me that I wasn't entirely at fault, it's difficult to absolve myself of blame after being the one to utter the words that unleashed a three-headed dog, resulting in the theft of countless souls within the town. The haunting images revealed by Causidol demonstrated the devastating impact of my actions on our families. Witnessing my father's valiant efforts to rescue people from a burning building, only to be confronted by Cerberus, was particularly distressing. I realized that I needed to compose myself and collaborate with Causidol rather than working against her. "I deeply apologize,

Causidol; I didn't intend to come across as impolite. The juxtaposition of seeing you and hearing the tale of the Gods engaging in a battle against Hades with the assistance of Merlin gives me the sensation of being trapped in a sinister fairy tale as if I'm about to awaken from a nightmare." These weren't empty words—everything felt like a twisted fairy tale with malevolent forces at play. Causidol scrutinized me for a moment before resuming the conversation.

"I believe it's important to recall this story because it reminds us that none of us have the kind of magical abilities possessed by Merlin. As a result, we'll need to rely on alternative methods. If we decide to utilize Latin for the incantation, it's likely to function more as a curse than a typical spell. Should we choose this course of action, you

need to be prepared to sacrifice something of value in order to seal Cerberus."

"Wait, hold on, I have to give something up. What are you talking about?" I asked in a panic. Causidol began to speak again.

"Merlin, being a powerful sorcerer, could simply tap into his magic to cast spells. However, since you don't possess enough magic to cast a spell, we'll have to resort to using a curse. The peculiar thing about curses is that they don't require magic; instead, you need to sacrifice something of great personal value to activate the incantation. So, Emma Harris, I have to inquire: what are you willing to give up in order to protect everyone?"

Heading back towards the elevator to regroup with Sophia, I became singularly fixated on the task at hand. The newfound information I had garnered filled me with a glimmer of hope for our mission. As I turned the corner, my path was abruptly blocked by a series of bookcases that had collapsed across the aisle. Puzzled by their sudden state, I couldn't shake the thought that I might have narrowly escaped being crushed by them. With no time to dwell, I sought out an alternate route. While dashing through the maze of shelves, the pressing question of whether we would have enough time to procure the item mentioned in the book continued to weigh heavily on my mind. Despite Causidol's reassurance of a two-hour timeframe and our decision to divide and conquer, I remained skeptical about the feasibility of our plan.

As I turned the corner, I found myself standing in front of the prop closet, a hidden treasure trove filled with various props for the library's displays. I contemplated whether they might have the type of chain I needed and decided it was worth the risk to search for it there, considering our time constraints. However, when I tried to open the door, I discovered it was locked. Frustrated but determined, I took a few steps back and then rushed to the door, throwing my shoulder into it. The door flew open, and as I stumbled inside, I found myself face-to-face with a creepy clown puppet. I let out a startled scream, grateful that no one was around to witness my reaction.

As I struggled to get back on my feet, I found myself in a spacious storage room filled with shelves stocked with an assortment of props. I meticulously scanned the room, half-expecting to encounter eerie, lifeless figures with gray eyes, but the room was vacant. Feeling a sense of relief, I cautiously explored the area. Among the items, I came across props suitable for the 4th of July, Halloween, and Christmas. Then, I stumbled upon artificial wildlife props, including birds and bears. After shifting aside a box of nutcrackers, I unearthed a large container labeled "Medieval Times." This discovery piqued my interest, and I eagerly ripped off the tape and delved into the contents of the box.

After rummaging through the box, I came across replica coins, scrolls, potion bottles, figurines, and other seemingly insignificant items. As I continued to sift through the contents, a faint jingling sound caught my attention. Ignoring the rest of the items, I focused on the source of the sound. Finally, my fingers closed around something familiar and cold - a three-foot-long black iron chain with oval-shaped links. Relief flooded through me as I realized that this was the missing ingredient needed to seal the book shut, preventing anyone from opening it again. Carefully setting aside the now unnecessary book, I cradled the heavy chain in my hands, unwilling to risk losing it. Glancing around the storage room, I quietly expressed my gratitude to an unknown benefactor who had led me to this crucial discovery.

As I left the storage room, I encountered another obstacle blocking my path. This time, it was a series of toppled bookcases, clearly moved by someone rather than just falling over. I pondered who could possibly be responsible for this, considering that most of the people around me seemed to be in a state of eerie stillness, resembling motionless zombies. It also struck me that the usual unsettling sound of howling yawns had been absent for some time.

I gazed down at the motionless figures sprawled across the ground, trying my best to block out the sight. They lay silent, their eyes shut and their bodies unnervingly still. Walking over to a man with a smooth, bald scalp and sun-kissed yellow skin adorned in a sweater vest, a crisp dress shirt, and khaki pants, I knelt beside him to examine him more closely. As I leaned in, his eyelids suddenly flew open, startling me. I instinctively rose to my feet and took a few steps backward. To my disbelief, the man began to rise to his feet as well. I couldn't fathom what I was witnessing. His back was turned to me, and a surge of hope washed over me as I entertained the possibility that perhaps not everyone had perished.

"Hey, are you okay? Do you know what's going on?" I asked, trying to keep my distance. The man remained unresponsive. I asked again, but still, there was no movement from him. I wondered if he was just trying to steady himself or if he was still half-asleep. "Hey, buddy, if you can hear me, can you turn around?" I said, hoping to get his attention. Regrettably, as soon as

I saw him turn to face me, I wished I hadn't asked. His eyes slowly opened, and to my horror, they were a piercing yellow with a red hue around them. A terrifying smile began to spread across his face, from ear to ear.

I stepped back, and the man advanced toward me. ***"So Causidol hid you in the void to prevent me from finding you. Clever girl, but no one can escape me,"*** the man said in a deep, menacing voice. I continued to back away as he steadily moved forward. "Who are you, and what do you mean by the void?" I asked, cautiously assessing my options for an escape route.

As the man approached me, he declared, ***"I am the breeder of fear, the stealer of souls, the guardian of the gates*** *to the underworld, the proud servant of Hades; I am Cerberus."* I stood my ground and retorted, "You may be Cerberus, but Causidol shielded us from you." The man halted and sneered, *"She may have placed you kids in a void to stop me from finding you, but my power is greater than hers now. I will find you and your souls will be mine,"* with a wicked grin on his face.

"How are you here, and how are you controlling this guy?" I asked, racking my brain for a way to escape. *"This human soul belongs to me, and so does his body. But not just his,"* he replied ominously. As he spoke, my thoughts of escape faded as I witnessed the lifeless bodies lying on the ground begin to stir. To my horror, a dozen people rose with piercing yellow eyes fixed on me, surrounding me in a menacing circle.

As I found myself in a perilous situation, my heart raced with fear. With my back pressed against the wall, I noticed the group of eerie, yellow-eyed individuals beginning to approach me, and a sense of urgency consumed my thoughts. Instinctively, I knew I had to flee. I made a daring move, swiftly maneuvering through the tightly packed crowd by slipping between someone's legs, narrowly evading their grasp. As I sprinted towards a row of toppled bookcases, I summoned every ounce of strength in my legs and leaped with determination. The memories of all those days spent struggling to ride my bike up steep hills suddenly seemed worthwhile as I managed to propel myself over the obstacle.

After landing, I wasted no time and swiftly continued my escape. Glancing back for a moment, I witnessed the menacing, yellow-eyed figures surmounting the bookcase in pursuit. Refusing to be deterred, I fixed my gaze forward and pushed myself to sprint even faster.

As I raced through the chaos, I couldn't shake the image of every person on the ground awakening with unnerving yellow eyes. Their outstretched hands grasped for me, but I ignored them, my singular focus on reaching Sophia before Cerberus found her. The taunting voice of Cerberus echoed in my mind, urging me on as I pushed myself to move even faster, desperate to outpace the looming threat.

"Laim Paker," all the yellowed-eyed figures echoed in unison, their synchronized voices sending shivers down my spine. ***"Will you make it in time?"*** The words seemed to hang in the air, heightening my sense of urgency. Despite Cerberus's attempts to distract me, I remained steadfast. "Hold on, Sophia, I'm coming."

I was taken aback by Causidol's request. When she first told me about saying a few words in Latin, there was no mention of having to sacrifice something. I felt confused and frustrated. "Why are you bringing this up now, Causidol? You never mentioned this before." I couldn't understand why she had only revealed this now.

"The reason I didn't bring it up earlier was because I wasn't sure if you were capable of handling it. However, time is of the essence, and it's crucial that we contain Cerberus once again. Are you prepared to take the necessary action?"

I didn't want to understand what she meant, but I knew what she was talking about. Throughout history, people had to give something to get something. But what do I hold most dear? "So I have to sacrifice myself because I don't have anything else?"

"No, you cannot sacrifice yourself since you are the one casting the spell. It must be someone else."

"Wait, did she really mention someone else?" I asked myself, feeling a sense of unease. "Causidol, who are you asking me to sacrifice? You can't possibly be referring to my father or my friends." Causidol remained silent, refusing to respond, and suddenly, it dawned on me. "You want the others out of the way so that I would have to choose which one of my friends to sacrifice!"

"You must make a decision quickly before it's too late. This is not a task for the faint of heart. Who among your friends will choose to save the world and reseal Cerberus in its prison?"

She seems completely serious. I would never consider that course of action. There must be another solution. Perhaps we could find an alternative, like using a chicken or some other method. "Causidol, why did you save my friends then? You could have simply allowed them to remain in that frozen state we were all in if you wanted me to use them to seal Cerberus," I inquired. But then, a sudden realization struck me. "You only saved them so you could manipulate them! You were aware from the beginning that this is what we would have to do. How could you be so cruel, so devoid of compassion?"

The air became thinner, and a mysterious green smoke began to swirl around me. Causidol's eyes emitted a brilliant, blinding glow, forcing me to cover my eyes with my hands. As Causidol began to levitate off the ground, a profound sense of terror consumed my entire being.

"Understand that my sole purpose is to keep Cerberus locked away from the world! You have the choice to help me complete my mission, or I will make the choice for you! I possess enough power to ensure that you

comply and fulfill the spell. Do not challenge me!"

The word "Causidol" echoed in my mind, causing me to collapse to the ground, overwhelmed by its power. "OK, I will choose; just please stop," I pleaded. As soon as I agreed, the deafening noise ceased, and the thick smoke began to dissipate. Causidol floated gently to the ground as I slowly rose to my feet. "So, what do I need to say to activate the spell?"

*"After your friends have obtained the necessary information and the book, all you need to say is, **'Cerberus libro vincietur et in aeternum obsignabitur. Liam sacrifico ut hanc maledictionem activem.'** (Cerberus will be bound by this book and sealed away for all eternity. I sacrifice Liam to activate this curse.)' Once you*

receive the additional information, you will need to add and modify the wording accordingly."

So, Causidol picked Liam. I bet she wasn't really going to give me a choice. I'm not going through with this by any means, but I will just play along while I think of something else. "Causidol, how much time do we have before Cerberus wakes up?"

Causidol remained silent, but her gaze shifted past me toward the doorway. I followed her line of sight and was startled to see a short white woman with brown hair, dressed in a sharp business suit, standing at the entrance. A sinister grin played on her lips as she tilted her head, partially obscuring her eyes with her hair. ***"Causidol, clever as always to hide these children in the void, but you knew I would***

track them down eventually," she declared in a menacing, deep voice. When she raised her head, her eyes glowed with a haunting yellow light, tinged with a menacing red hue.

I'm almost there; just hoping Sophia is all right. The overwhelming sense of safety made me momentarily forget the exhaustion creeping up on me. More of the yellow-eyed pursuers were drawing closer, but my heightened senses kept me on edge. I had to reach Sophia because I couldn't shake the feeling that there might be something more between us, a sense that we could be more than just friends. I had never imagined being with someone like her in my life. She was intelligent, humorous, and undeniably beautiful. Today, after every-thing that has unfolded, I feel compelled to take the risk and inquire if she feels the same way. The memory of the day we first met is still vivid in my mind.

It had only been a few days since Emma and I first met at school. We quickly be-came close friends, especially since we both felt a little out of place. However, one day, she surprised me by saying she wanted to introduce me to her other friend, Sophia. I had no idea that it was going to be Sophia, the girl whose mother is the mayor and whose father is the police captain. There I was, standing in the cafeteria with my unappetizing school lunch, and I saw the most beautiful girl I had ever met. At that moment, I instantly knew that a guy like me didn't stand a chance with her.

Emma motioned for me to join her at the table, and as I approached, I felt a surge of nervousness. I sat down, keeping my head low, not wanting Sophia to see my insecurity. Surprisingly, Sophia greeted me warmly and complimented my glasses, which filled me with pure joy. She treated me kindly, never getting upset when I was late or preoccupied with my next video edit. Despite this, I still felt like I didn't belong, especially when I attended a community event and observed the type of men associated with someone of Sophia's social standing - affluent, towering, and handsome. I didn't fit that description at all. Despite my insecurities, something was different today. I felt an unprecedented courage, a desire to protect my friends and support my family. If this newfound bravery persisted, I resolved to confess my feelings to Sophia at the end of the day.

I dashed away from the person trying to grab me, vaulting over them as I continued running. I hurdled yet another toppled bookcase, finally reaching the meet-up spot. However, my relief was short-lived as I was greeted by the unsettling sight of fifty people with piercing yellow eyes standing in the open area in front of the elevator. Across from them, Sophia loomed atop a tower of fallen bookcases, observing others as they began to climb.

As I stood at the top of the toppled-over bookcase, I looked down and saw a chilling scene unfolding below. Around fifty eerie figures with wicked grins and bright yellow eyes were gathered, all staring up at me. Their voices merged into a bone-chilling chorus as they warned, ***"You will not escape me."*** A shiver ran down my spine, and I realized that there was no way I could climb down from where I was. The unsettling part was that these figures seemed to be more concerned with keeping me trapped than actually advancing towards me.

As I held the Bible in my trembling hands, I felt it slipping, and I quickly adjusted my grip. Suddenly, the expressions on the faces of the yellow-eyed figures changed, and their smiles vanished. In unison, they demanded to know, ***"What do you think you're going to do with that book?"*** I chose to remain silent, holding the book tightly.

Their demand shifted to a furious command as they all shouted, ***"Give me that book."*** Within moments, about five of them started to swarm the toppled bookcase, scrambling toward me with a menacing determination. Panic surged through me as I scrambled to devise a plan, knowing that I had to act fast.

As I scanned the scene, a surge of calmness washed over me when I caught Liam in my peripheral vision. He wore a serious expression, his eyes focused on the unfolding events. I couldn't help but feel reassured by his presence. However, as I glanced back at him, he had vanished. Panic began to well up inside me, questioning whether his earlier display of bravery was merely an act. Just as despair threatened to consume me, the thundering sound of footsteps against metal drew my attention. To my amazement, I saw Liam racing atop the metal bookshelves, determined and fearless. With a mighty leap, he landed on a bookcase positioned just below me and directly above one of the menacing yellow-eyed climbers. With a decisive kick, he sent a bookcase toppling onto two of the climbers. I watched in disbelief as they rose unharmed, unfazed by the impact.

Liam ascended to my level, and as soon as he reached the top, I enveloped him in a tight hug. "Thank you," I murmured, my face pressed into his shoulder. He held me close and reassured me, "I'll always be here for you. But right now, we need to find a way out of this situation." I pulled away from the embrace and surveyed our surroundings. Menacing yellow-eyed figures stood before us, and when I glanced back at the path we had just climbed, more of them were beginning to ascend. Liam's focused expression indicated that he was searching for an escape route. I couldn't shake the thought from my mind—was this the end for us?

"Who's that at the door, Causidol?" I inquired, my gaze locked with the woman who seemed fixated on me. Causidol said nothing, simply continuing to stare at the doorway. Not wanting to wait for Causidol's response, I addressed the woman directly. "Hello, I'm Emma. Are you okay? Your eyes are a striking bright yellow." The woman remained motionless, not uttering a word. I repeated my question to Causidol, asking for the identity of the mysterious lady.

"Cerberus has gained control of the bodies he extracted souls from. I never expected him to achieve this level of power so quickly. He must be at or near full strength now. Where are your friends, Emma? We are running out of time."

"Causidol, I have a question," I said, my mind racing. You told us Cerberus was sleeping and that we had two hours. You also said you were shielding us from him. So, why is he here now? It hasn't been two hours. What's going on?" Panic started to set in as I thought about what could be happening to Sophia and Liam if Cerberus was able to reach us.

"Haha, Causidol, you lied to her and her friends. Why not tell them you placed them in the void? No matter, I will take them now," the lady said with a menacing voice. Her words filled me with even more nervousness about what could be happening to my friends. Another concern was what this mysterious mention of Causidol not telling the truth and the void meant. But at that moment, my priority was figuring out how to bypass the lady and reach my friends.

"Emma, be prepared to run. I will create an opening."

Causidol confidently raised her hand, and a brilliant green light materialized in her palm. With a swift motion, she aimed her hand at the lady, and a dazzling burst of light shot forth, propelling the lady away from the door. Without hesitation, I dashed out of the club, following the path that Liam and Sophia had taken. Little did I know that a new challenge awaited me. As I turned the corner, a group of menacing, yellow-eyed figures stood in my way. Suddenly, a protective green mist enveloped me, causing the attackers to recoil as if repelled by an invisible force. Without pausing to see if the mist would linger, I pressed on, fleeing from the unsettling scene.

The sound of my footsteps echoed through the dimly lit hallway as I hurried along. I glanced back to see people attempting to approach me, only to recoil as they were repelled by the eerie green mist surrounding me. As I reached the stairs, I was met with a sight that made my heart sink - the staircase had caved in, blocking my path. How had Sophia and Liam made it to the second floor? The answer became clear as my eyes fell upon the elevator. A tall, imposing figure was pounding on the control panel, causing the elevator doors to shudder. As I approached, the figure stopped and turned to face me, his yellow eyes glinting with malice as a sinister grin spread across his face.

As I stood there, it became evident that I wouldn't be using the elevator anytime soon. Hastily, I dashed over to the railing to peer down at the second floor, hoping to catch a glimpse of them. Reaching the edge, I leaned over and scanned the area below. My eyes fell upon a chaotic scene - shelves of books knocked over and a small fire burning in the distance. Amidst the disarray, I finally spotted them - my dear friends Liam and Sophia, perched on top of a pile of bookcases, peering down at a group of menacing figures with yellowed eyes, gradually ascending towards them. It was a heartening sight, yet it also filled me with trepidation.

The green mist enveloped me as I desperately searched for Causidol without any success. Realizing that I couldn't wait any longer, I knew I had to reach my friends. As I scanned my surroundings, my eyes landed on a banner hanging on the wall decorated with illustrations of books. Without hesitation, I hurried over to it and tore it off the wall. I swiftly secured one end of the banner to the railing and wrapped the other end around my hand, ensuring a firm grip. Stepping back, I took a moment to gather my thoughts, offered a quick prayer, and then took a deep breath before dashing towards the edge.

I dashed forward and propelled myself over the edge. As I hurtled through the air, I held my breath, praying that the banner would bear my weight. Suddenly, I collided with the end of the banner, triggering a resounding pop as I swung toward the second floor. Releasing my grip on the banner, I crashed to the ground in a daze. Before me, a group of people with striking yellow eyes was rapidly approaching. I feared the worst, but just then, the mysterious green mist reappeared, sending the figure hurtling backward. Still feeling disoriented from my daring maneuver, I struggled to my feet and frantically searched for my friends. There they were, perched atop the bookcases, surrounded by the yellow-eyed individuals. With the protective green mist at my command, I knew I could rescue them.

Chapter 9
Cerberus

I swiftly shut the heavy wooden door and turned the lock with a shiver running down my spine. The sight of Cerberus lurking outside made me wish I could crawl under my bed and never come out. Liam and Sophia were perched on the edge of the worn-out couch, their chests heaving as they struggled to regain their breath. My own breath came in ragged gasps, a testament to the frantic sprint we had just escaped from. I couldn't help but notice the Bible clutched tightly in Sophia's trembling hands while Liam had an iron chain wound around his clenched fist. I understood why Sophia held the Bible, but the purpose of the iron chain eluded me. Walking over to the window, I cautiously peeked through the closed blinds, still able to make out Cerberus's menacing silhouette prowling through the park. The Causidol Green Mist continued to shield us from his searching gaze. I drew the blinds shut and made my way to my father's worn armchair, sinking into its comforting embrace.

"Okay, I think we are safe for the moment. But I don't think Causidol can hide us for long. What did you guys find out at the library?" I asked. Sophia straightened up and said, "This Old Testament Bible should be a good replacement." Liam let go of the chain and set it on the coffee table. "I read in a book that chains can help bind monsters. I found this chain in the prop room before those yellow-eyed people found me. I was thinking if you use this chain in the spell, then we can lock the book in chains where no one could open it again. I'm not sure if it would work, so maybe Causidol could answer that. But where did she go?" Liam said. We all looked around, but we couldn't see her. I called out for her, and we got a response.

"I cannot reveal myself in the same way as before while we're hiding from Cerberus. I am by your side, and Liam is right - the plan will succeed. You have all the components required. It's now time to face Cerberus and put an end to this never-ending struggle. Emma, you are aware of what needs to be done."

Causidol's voice reverberated through the house as if the very walls were speaking. However, I wasn't prepared to rush out and confront the impending apocalypse without getting some answers first. I still had lingering questions. "Causidol, as I mentioned earlier, we won't take any action until you provide us with some explanations. What exactly is this 'void' that Cerberus mentioned? And what changed, considering we were told that we had two hours due to Cerberus being asleep?" After a long silence, Causidol finally spoke.

"I must admit that I wasn't truthful when I claimed that Cerberus was asleep. In reality, it was as if you were the ones in a slumber, oblivious to the danger around you. When Cerberus broke free, it consumed your essence. Fortunately, I managed to re-

trieve you and restore you to your physical forms. Although it may have appeared that I banished Cerberus in its weakened state when we confronted it directly, I actually transported us to safety. I relocated us to a timeless void, where time passed much more slowly than in the real world. While we conversed in your clubroom, what felt like mere minutes to you actually equated to hours passing for everyone else."

"I provided the two-hour deadline, hoping that Cerberus would weaken and take longer to regain his strength after his release. However, I miscalculated, and he recovered much faster than I expected. Although he managed to locate your children through the void, he is still vulnerable to the magic left within me by Merlin. When he attempted to exert his influence through the souls *he had taken, I resisted due to the magic's protection. As my barrier is on the verge of breaking, it's imperative that we act swiftly, as he will undoubtedly stop at nothing to find you once he learns of your plan to seal him again."*

A surge of emotions overwhelmed me in an instant. Anger, sorrow, and anguish churned within me as I realized the gravity of the situation. Despite our presence, people were suffering, and we were oblivious to it. Causidol revealed the fate of our parents, but what we witnessed was the aftermath of events that had transpired hours, if not days, earlier. Tears cascaded down my cheeks as I imagined my father lying helplessly in the streets while I was engrossed in a dispute with a spirit. Liam rose to his feet and bellowed, "How could you! You had no right!" Sophia, too, stood up and shouted, "My parents were abandoned without any knowledge of my whereabouts because of you! Why didn't you save everyone? Why only us?"

Causidol remained silent, and her lack of response confirmed my suspicions. It became clear to me that she had only sought us out because of my ability to speak Latin. She had no regard for us as individuals; we were merely tools to help her achieve her own objectives. I could see that my friends, Liam and Sophia, felt the same way. However, we all understood that this situation was much larger than Causidol alone. Our families, the town, and ultimately, the entire world depended on us to take action.

"Causidol, if you had just told us the truth from the beginning, you wouldn't have lost all of our trust," I said before the ringing sound of agony echoed loudly in my head. I covered my ears and collapsed to the ground, screaming in agony. Liam and Sophia rushed to my side, but the noise was so intense that it was blinding. Amidst the cacophony, I could make out Causidol's voice.

"Emma Harris, I refuse to answer your questions or be interrogated by you and your friends. I am the Keeper of the Book of Cerberus. I have watched over him long before you were born. I may not have been honest, but you lack the willpower to carry out my plan. You lack what is needed for this mission, and I knew only your friends would give you the motivation you need to carry out my plan. But I am growing impatient. You are taking too long, and Cerberus will

open the Gates of Hades soon. You must go now. If you don't confront Cerberus and end this mayhem, I will show this pain to your friends. Don't waste any more time. Also, be prepared to sacrifice one of your friends for the curse. Don't think I forgot that you never chose one of them. If you don't choose, I will choose for you."

The deafening noise finally subsided, and with Liam's help, I managed to stand back up. My head was pounding, making it difficult to think straight. "What just happened?" Liam asked, but his words barely registered due to the lingering effects of the intense sound. I informed them that Causidol was impatient and wanted us to go after Cerberus. However, I couldn't bring myself to disclose Causidol's true intentions regarding sacrificing one of them.

How could I ask one of them to sacrifice themselves to rectify my mistake? Time was running out, but I was desperately searching for another solution.

"Hey guys, I want to remind you of our conversation earlier. We've got everything we need, but I won't pretend that I'm not scared or that I don't want to run and hide. It's just us left, and I don't want to spend my life living in fear. If any of you want to stay behind, I completely understand." I was about to say more when Sophia playfully hit me on the arm. "Are you out of your mind? We started this together and we're going to finish it tonight. You're not going through this alone, and I know that Liam feels the same way. I want my parents back, and I know you want your dad back, while Liam wants his mom and sister

back. You're not getting rid of us that easily. We're in this together." Sophia's words
were met with a nod from Liam and a triumphant fist pump in the air. I couldn't
ask for better friends.

Liam Queston voiced our mutual concern about how to confront Cerberus, emphasizing that sneaking up on him wasn't
a feasible option. With so much going on,
I was struggling to come up with a plan.
Just then, Sophia proposed an idea. She
suggested that Causidol conceal us in mist
until we reached an open area in the park,
specifically the space in front of the pond
by the statue. This location would provide enough room for us to draw Cerberus out into the open, especially considering his increased size. The plan involved
placing the Bible and the chain on the

ground, after which I would recite the spell to seal Cerberus. Once everything was set, Causidol would release mist, prompting Cerberus to move toward me. Meanwhile, Liam and Sophia would be nearby, also concealed by mist, prepared to support as needed. Sophia then asked Causidol if this plan would work for them.

"I concur with your proposed course of action. Let's move swiftly, as time is not in our favor."

After Causidol approved Sophia's plan, we knew it was time to face Cerberus and rescue our family. I grabbed the Bible and the chain, and with determination, I rallied everyone, declaring, "It's time to go hunting."

As I watched Emma come to the realization that she couldn't handle this challenge alone, I felt a wave of relief, knowing that we would face it together. Though fear still lingered, there was no time to dwell on it. Emma declared that it was time to go hunting, and Liam enthusiastically echoed her battle cry. The bond between these two friends was evident, and I felt grateful to have them by my side. Emma was one of the few people who truly understood me, and the events of the day had given me a newfound appreciation for Liam. While I had always liked him, he now exuded a sense of maturity and self-assurance. Even Emma seemed to have grown after the bold move she pulled at the library. I knew I had to contribute something, and I hoped that my plan would bring us success.

Emma picked up the Bible and the chain, feeling the weight of their significance in her hands, and walked purposefully over to the door. As she turned the doorknob, a sense of determination filled her. Liam silently followed behind her, and I brought up the rear, feeling the hair on the back of my neck stand on end.

She glanced back at us, seeking assurance, and I gave her a nod, signaling that we were ready. With resolute determination, she pushed the door open, revealing the eerie sight of the green mist still swirling around the house. I closed the door firmly behind us, instinctively scanning the thick fog for any sign of Cerberus, but the dense mist obscured everything beyond a few feet.

"Could this be Cerberus's doing?" I inquired, and Emma's grave expression confirmed my suspicion. Liam wisely proposed that we stay close to each other as we made our way to the statue, a suggestion Emma and I unanimously agreed to. As we set off from the house, the green mist ominously enveloped us, creating an otherworldly atmosphere as we ventured toward the park.

As we proceeded cautiously, we scanned our surroundings for any indication of Cerberus. It was almost unbelievable that we couldn't spot him, considering his immense size comparable to that of a cruise ship. The fog grew denser with every step we took. I reached for Liam's hand, and he grasped Emma's shoulder with his other hand. We were determined not to lose each other in the thick fog. Fortunately, Emma's familiarity with the park reassured us that we wouldn't risk getting separated.

As we were walking through the thick fog, Emma suddenly halted and asked if I felt it, too. I looked around, and although I couldn't see anything through the dense fog, I couldn't shake off the feeling of being watched from above. It felt like Cerberus was lurking much closer than we had anticipated, perhaps right above us. Despite the unsettling sensation, Liam urged us to continue. As Emma led the way, assuring us that we were almost there, the pressure of the eerie feeling grew more intense with every step. It was as if an unseen presence was looming above, waiting for us to halt. Despite this unnerving sensation, we persevered and continued moving forward. Finally, Emma stopped and proclaimed that we had arrived. Through the fog, I could make out the imposing statue of a warrior lady standing right in front of us.

"Alright, it's time to get this over with," Emma announced with determination. As she pointed to a massive rock on the left and a sturdy tree on the right, she instructed, "You guys go hide, and I'll get this set up."

Following her orders, Liam and I swiftly dispersed. However, as we moved away from Emma, an eerie mist began trailing behind me, enveloping both Liam and me in its swirling tendrils. Taking cover behind the rugged rock, I knelt down while Liam sought refuge behind the wide trunk of the tree.

Meanwhile, Emma knelt down and carefully arranged the Bible on the ground, encircling it with a chain. It was evident that she was being guided by some unseen force, perhaps Causidol. As she finished her task, she stood up and glanced at both Liam and me. We responded with a thumbs-up, eliciting a smile from Emma. After taking a deep breath, the green mist began to dissipate, leaving Emma standing in front of the statue with no spiritual protection.

As the mist dissipated, the fog began to clear, revealing a colossal being towering over Emma. With three ominous heads poised to strike, it loomed larger than a battleship. I felt as though my feet were encased in concrete, paralyzed by the fear rising within me as I witnessed my friend confronting this unholy creature face-to-face.

As Sophia and Liam sought shelter behind the enormous rock and the broad tree, I knelt down and consulted Causidol on how to position the book and chains. She advised me to place the Bible on the ground and encircle it with the chain. Following her instructions, I did as she said, then stood back up to exchange a reassuring glance with Sophia and Liam. They both signaled their approval with a thumbs-up, and I couldn't help but smile. Their presence gave me the strength I needed; I couldn't have faced this challenge alone.

Taking a deep breath, I thought about the people for whom I was undertaking this task: Sophia's mom and dad, Liam's mother and sister, and, of course, my own dad. Despite our differences since my mom's passing, I still cared deeply for him. I reminded myself of the purpose driving me forward.

Finally, I instructed Causidol to dispel the mist. As I spoke, the mist began to dissipate, and the fog gradually lifted. Previously, I could barely see five feet ahead, but now an enormous, ominous black, three-headed dog materialized before me as the fog cleared, as though it had been waiting for me to dispel the green mist.

Cerberus had undergone a dramatic transformation. No longer the skinny, three-headed dog of yore, he now stood tall and imposing, towering over the city like a skyscraper. His massive body was packed with thick, sinewy muscles, his legs powerful and sturdy, surpassing the height of any building in town. His fur, a deep and lustrous black, billowed in the wind, resembling tendrils of black fire flickering around him. His teeth, gleaming a bright, incandescent yellow, shone like the evening sun at its fullest. As he opened his jaws, a river of saliva cascaded to the ground, sizzling and igniting everything it touched. His three heads, once slender and elongated, now exuded an air of formidable strength and presence.

They were large and had a resemblance to that of a jackal, with sharp pointed ears. On each of its heads, there were a pair of horns that looked like they belonged to mountain goats. It was a sight of pure fear that overwhelmed my whole body, but what sent terror down to my very core was its eyes. An ominous yellow color that brought everything that I was ever afraid of back to the surface of my mind. I was frozen; I couldn't move; I couldn't breathe. I was like the very statue that stood behind me.

"So you finally show yourself to me, little one. Do you think you could hide from me forever? I saw you enter your home and decided to wait for you to come to me. I could have gotten to you sooner, but I relish the fact that you believe you have any hope of stopping me from releasing my master. Hades will rise, and with me by his side, the

world as you know it will be gone. But you will watch as your soul will be me. Causidol should have picked better, but now all she can do is watch and place blame on her master for punishing her to watch over me. Oh, how I longed for this day."

As I heard Cerberus speak about punishing Causidol, confusion washed over me. Cerberus noticed my perplexed expression and burst into laughter, sounding like a hyena.

"Did she not tell you? Causidol was once a witch who did horrible deeds to innocent people. Merlin stopped her and, as punishment, made her the keeper of me. Her soul will only last as long as I'm imprisoned. The longer I'm out, the more she fades away. That's

why she wants me back in the book, so she can live on. She might have told you a lie about saving the world, but she only wants to save herself."

As Cerberus' raucous laughter echoed, my mind raced back to all the words Causidol had spoken. I realized that her professed goal of saving everyone and thwarting Cerberus' plan to release Hades was nothing but a deceitful ploy to save herself. Every word she uttered was a lie, and now she was expecting me to rescue her by sacrificing one of my friends. I had been completely duped from the beginning, falling for her deception like a naive fool.

As I gazed out of the corner of my eye, I noticed the green mist surrounding Sophia beginning to dissipate. Panic surged through me, and I shouted at

Causidol to restore the mist, but she paid no heed to my pleas. Meanwhile, Cerberus shifted its three heads in Sophia's direction. Paralyzed, I found myself unable to move, even though Cerberus was no longer fixated on me. Upon looking down, I spotted wisps of green smoke ensnaring my feet, a clear sign of Causidol's control over me. Despite being coerced by Causidol, I was determined not to carry out her bidding, yet time was running out, and I was without a plan.

In an instant, a rock struck Cerberus directly in one of its eyes, causing the three-headed creature to whip its heads around to find the source of the projectile. To everyone's surprise, it was Liam, standing unwavering and determined, with another rock in his hand, poised to let it fly. His eyes betrayed no hint of fear as he boldly faced off against the formidable Cerberus. I stood there in absolute astonishment, observing Liam fearlessly confront the monstrous beast.

As the mist surrounding Sophia vanished, Cerberus turned his menacing gaze towards her. Feeling a surge of adrenaline, I knew I couldn't just stand by. Gripping a handful of rocks, I called out to Causidol, demanding the mist around me dissipate. Summoning all my strength, I emerged from behind the safety of the tree, determined to confront the formidable Cerberus. With a swift, powerful throw, I aimed for his eye, causing him to redirect his attention towards me, his three heads now fixated on my presence.

Sophia and Emma were both staring at me, yelling for me to stop, but I just couldn't. It might have been the most reckless decision I've ever made, but after everything I had gone through for my friends today, especially for Sophia, the fear of rejection from her vanished as I realized she was the one for me. I wasn't willing to lose her to a monster, not now, not ever. If this was going to be my final stand, I was going to make it count.

"Hey, you big mutt. You think I'm scared of you? You've never met my sister. You're going back to prison, and you're going to release our families," I said with every bit of courage left in my body.

"Ah, another challenger and this one seems bold. I remember when we first met at the library, and I could sense your courage. I am looking forward to this. Come at me with all your strength, my dear opponent."

As I prepared to hurl another rock, a brilliant green light suddenly burst forth, illuminating the surroundings. In the midst of the radiance, I beheld Emma, her arm held aloft and her eyes aglow with a vivid green hue.

Liam must have lost his mind as he marched down Cerberus, shouting at him. Why couldn't he have just stayed hidden behind the tree? I glanced back at Sophia and saw her beginning to rise, determined to rush over to Liam. I urgently told her not to move, but she seemed oblivious to my plea. Ignoring my warning, she sprang to sprint towards Liam. Panic gripped me as I prepared to witness my friends dashing into potential danger. Overwhelmed, I beseeched Causidol to grant me power. Suddenly, a burst of green light enveloped me, and I felt the energy coursing through my entire body. Raising my hands, I was about to act until I recalled Causidol's words from the clubroom: "It doesn't have to be someone you care about; you just need a sacrifice to activate the curse." I knew what I had to do; I just hoped it wasn't too late.

I began to speak in Latin. ***"Cerberus in hac Biblia ferreis catenis ligata sigilletur. Spiritum Causidol sarifico ut hoc maleficium exsequar."*** (Cerberus be sealed in this Bible bound by iron chains.

I sacrifice the spirit Causidol in order to perform this curse)

I could still hear Causidol's desperate yell resounding in my head, a fruitless warning, as it turned out. The vibrant green energy that had enveloped me now dispersed around the ancient Bible lying on the ground. Slowly, almost eerily, the book began to levitate, its pages unfurling in the direction of Cerberus. The chain, previously encircling me, detached itself and was swiftly consumed by the mystical tome as it snapped shut, catching Cerberus off guard.

Cerberus swiftly pivoted in my direction, but before he could take any action, the book sprung open again. This time, ominous black chains shot out from its pages, entwining themselves around Cerberus' imposing form. Frantically, he tried to break free, but the chains held him in an unyielding grip.

I urgently called out to Sophia and Liam, urging them to make their way to my side. Without hesitation, they sprinted towards me, standing just behind my shoulder. Together, we bore witness to Cerberus' powers being steadily drained away. The chains seemed to constrict around him, inexorably siphoning his formidable strength. Bright white sparks emanated from his diminishing form, marking the expulsion of his once-unfathomable power.

Gradually, his immense figure dwindled, diminishing from the size of a battleship to that of a diminutive, feeble canine. Cerberus, now reduced to a fraction of his former self, appeared woefully enervated compared to the formidable force he had been upon his release.

As Cerberus, no bigger than my hand, struggled against the pull of the book, the chains yanked him forcefully. His attempts to resist were in vain as the relentless chains hoisted him into the air and drew him inexorably into the pages of the Bible. With a resounding thud, the book snapped shut and began to spin, engulfed by swirling black chains. Suddenly, a brilliant flash of green light illuminated the scene, and the book tumbled to the ground.

Chapter 10
Aftermath

I asked, "Is it over?" as we stood before the book that had swallowed Cerberus. It lay before us, wrapped in chains that seemed impossible to open without bolt cutters. I walked over to the ancient Bible and picked it up with both hands. The book felt warm as if something inside was struggling to break free but was trapped. I turned to my friends, and we all had the same question in our eyes. "I think we did it," I said confidently. Liam, looking around, asked, "But how do we know? I don't hear or see anyone." We all stood there, pondering if our efforts had saved anyone. Then, the sky began to clear, and sun rays pierced through the dark clouds, bringing back the bright blue sky. We all looked up, feeling the sun's warmth on our skin, a sensation we hadn't felt in a long time and thought we might never experience again. I closed my eyes, letting the sun's radiance wash over me until I heard a distant sound. Opening my eyes, I could hear people calling out, kids screaming and crying, and the sounds of police sirens and fire trucks roaring outside of the park.

We gazed into each other's eyes and let out a triumphant scream. Tears and laughter filled the air as we embraced, our collective relief palpable. The nightmare was finally over, and our efforts had saved the town. "Do you think those white sparks emanating from Cerberus were the souls he had taken?" Sophia inquired. I nodded in agreement. Her radiant smile lit up as she jubilantly exclaimed that we had done it. And she was right - we had indeed achieved the impossible. We had averted the end of the world. What was truly remarkable was that it wasn't the adults or the brave and courageous who had accomplished this feat. Instead, it was a group of outcasts, those whom everyone had ignored. As Sophia and Liam shared an embrace that seemed to convey more than just relief, I discreetly turned away to give them a moment of privacy. Gazing down at the book in my hands, I mused about what lay ahead.

"What are we going to do about that book?" Liam asked. His concern mirrored my own. I pondered a potential solution, but I wasn't sure if it would even work. Nevertheless, I took the book and walked over to the imposing statue of Athena. Placing the book before the goddess, I gazed up at her and spoke with conviction. "With the recent events unfolding, a previously unknown world has revealed itself to us. If gods and monsters truly exist, then perhaps this will work. Athena, Goddess of wisdom, I, Emma Harris, offer the Book of Cerberus to you as a tribute to watch over me, my friends, and our families."

Suddenly, an owl's hoot pierced the air. We turned to see a magnificent snow-white owl with striking silver eyes perched in the trees, seemingly watching us intently. It then spread its wings and gracefully took flight, leaving us in a state of wonder.

When I turned back to the statue, the Book of Cerberus had vanished.

"Well, I suppose that's that," Liam remarked. As a gentle breeze brushed past us, the park gradually filled with people seeking answers. I looked at my friends and suggested, "Let's head back to the clubroom."

The journey back to the library felt like navigating through a chaotic circus. The roads were bustling with people, paying no attention to who or what they were brushing past. Upon reaching the Library, we found it in complete disarray. Somehow, the elevator was still operational, and we managed to reach the third floor. Along the way, we encountered people who had been possessed just hours earlier, now looking bewildered and trying to make sense of what had transpired. Maneuvering through the confused crowd, we finally reached the clubroom. Although the door was missing, our belongings were intact inside. I quickly retrieved my backpack, and everyone else did the same.

I took a seat and finally settled in for a break, and Sophia did the same. Meanwhile, Liam remained standing as he rummaged through his bag and pulled out an old video camera. He gazed at it with a mixture of emotions. "What's wrong, Liam?" I inquired. He looked up and confessed, "This is my dad's old camera. He left it to me when he passed away. I never really used it, but after today, I never want to miss capturing something that could change the world. One day, I will become the greatest director in history." As he looked at us, he noticed our proud expressions and quickly added, "Sorry, I didn't mean to sound lame." Suddenly, Sophia stood up, walked over to him, and planted a kiss on his cheek. "I believe in you, and I'll be right there when it happens," she assured him. Liam's face turned bright red, a stark contrast to his dark complexion. I tried my best to keep quiet to avoid ruining their moment, but someone else ended up interrupting them.

A librarian stood at the door and told us we had to leave. We understood and grabbed our things. As we made our way out of the library, I told Liam and Sophia, "I'll see you later." They got on their bikes and waved goodbye. We all went our separate ways back home, hoping to see our families.

As I pedaled up the hill, I found my-self surprisingly nostalgic for this famil-iar yet challenging path. The chaos that surrounded me as I maneuvered through the streets was overwhelming. Abandoned cars littered the area, some carelessly parked on lawns and others obstructing the flow of traffic. I couldn't help but no-tice the bewildered expressions on people's faces as they tried to make sense of what had happened. All I could focus on was the urgent need to return home and en-sure my family's safety. Upon reaching my driveway, I dismounted my bike and ap-proached my house. Despite the unsettling sight of a burning tree in the front yard, the exterior of the house seemed relatively unscathed. As I neared the front door, it suddenly swung open, and I found myself enveloped in a tight embrace by my tearful mother.

As I lay on the floor, my mom sobbed over me, her eyes filled with tears. "I thought we lost you. We drove home after waking up at the cafe, thinking you were there. Liam, don't scare me like that again," she cried out. I wanted to tell her I was at the library, but at that moment, I didn't want to ruin the emotional intensity of the situation. "I told you he was fine," my sister said as she walked out of the house. Her voice betrayed her attempt to appear non-chalant as tears glistened in her eyes. I told her that I loved her too, and she immediately broke down, rushing over to hug me. The three of us stood in the front yard, wrapped in a tight embrace, with two out of the three of us crying uncontrollably. It was a moment filled with raw emotion as if we wouldn't see tomorrow. But I knew that because of what I and my friends had done, there would be a tomorrow.

I opened the front door with a mix of anticipation and trepidation, hoping to catch a glimpse of either my mom or dad. However, the eerie stillness inside suggested that no one was home. Stepping out onto the chaotic scene outside, I felt a wave of relief wash over me as I realized I was finally back in the safety of my own home. Surveying the aftermath, I noticed that the only damage to our property was a car that had careened into the pool house. It was clear that the driver had abandoned the vehicle and fled the scene. Taking a moment to collect my thoughts, I sank into the comforting embrace of the couch, grappling with the harsh reality of what had transpired. I longed for it all to be a terrible nightmare, but the cold truth hung heavy in the air. Just as I closed my eyes, the sound of the door creaking open shattered the stillness, accompanied by my mom's voice calling out to me.

I jumped up and dashed to the front door. When I turned the corner, I spotted my mom standing in the doorway. Our eyes met, and we both rushed towards each other. We wrapped our arms around each other in the middle of the hallway, holding each other tight. She told me she had been so worried and had hurried home as soon as she could. I asked her about dad, and she explained that he was out trying to restore order but would be back soon. I felt the urge to tell her everything that had transpired, but at that moment, I simply wanted-ed to savor the comfort of her embrace. As long as my parents were safe, nothing else mattered.

As I strolled through the park, I couldn't help but feel a sense of warmth as I watched families coming together. The sight of kids reuniting with their parents, overflowing with love and joy, was truly heartwarming. However, as I made my way home, I couldn't shake the thought that my own father wouldn't be there. He was likely still out, selflessly helping others.

Approaching the house, I braced myself for the empty silence that awaited me. Opening the door, I was met with an eerie quiet that confirmed my fears. Just as I was about to resign myself to an empty home, a familiar voice boomed, "Emma, is that you?" I couldn't believe it. Was it really my dad? As he hurried into view and engulfed me in a tight embrace, all my worries melted away.

"I thought you would still be out there rescuing people," I managed to say between gasps for air. He released his grip on me, allowing me to catch my breath. Placing his hand on my face, he said, "You're the only person I was worried about saving. I went to the library, but you weren't there. I drove home, and you weren't here either. I was about to leave and go look for you." These words from my dad brought tears to my eyes. I never expected him to go to such lengths for me.

"I didn't think you were listening to me when I said I was going to the library. You never paid much attention to me before, so I just assumed you weren't going to be here," I said, feeling a mixture of frustration and sadness. He gently put his hand on my head and said, "I know after your mother passed, it seemed like I was pushing you away, but that wasn't the case. I wanted to make you more independent in case of the day I don't make it back home from work. Your mother was the love of my life, and I was supposed to leave before her, but life didn't have it that way. But you are my little girl, the one thing left in this world I hold dear, so of course, I listen to whatever you say and where you're going. I know I can't turn back time, but if I could, I would show you how much I love you, Emma." His words were too much to bear, and I couldn't hold it in. I leapt back into his arms and started to cry my eyes out. Despite my tears, I was incredibly grateful for this moment, knowing that there was a chance I would have never gotten this opportunity to truly understand his feelings.

Two months had passed, and the news was abuzz with reports about scientists investigating a peculiar storm that had swept through, releasing a mysterious gas that had put the entire town to sleep. It was a story that only regular folks like us could comprehend. My friends and I made a pact not to divulge the truth of what really happened, knowing we wouldn't be able to prove it. As summer raced by, the town was slowly being rebuilt. Luckily, the class project was canceled due to people still recovering from the aftermath of the so-called storm.

During the remaining summer days, Sophia, Liam, and I enjoyed watching movies, going on hikes, and swimming in Sophia's pool. Liam and Sophia grew closer, and finally, Liam gathered the courage to ask her out. The two were off on the cookie date they had been talking about for months. Meanwhile, I found solace in my room, writing down every detail of that unforgettable day.

With school looming just a few weeks away, I found myself apprehensive about returning to the whirlwind of high school life, especially with the presence of the mean girls, Ella, Victoria, and Chloe, who were trying to garner sympathy from our classmates. They claimed to have been the worst affected by the storm, despite the fact that their parents' cars had sustained the most damage. Yet, with school on the horizon, a small part of me was looking forward to returning to history class with Mr. Barnes.

Though summer was drawing to a close, I made a promise to savor this simple life. I never wanted to bear the weight of the world on my shoulders. For now, my only focus was navigating the challenges of high school.

EPILOGUE

October 13th, 2054

Today marks the thirty-year anniversary of the unforgettable day. It was the day when my closest friends, Liam, Sophia, and I faced the terrifying Cerberus, the three-headed dog, and managed to seal him away, thus preventing the end of the world. Despite the passage of time, people still recall it as the day when a powerful storm swept through, releasing strange gases that caused everyone to fall asleep. However, my friends and I knew the truth of what had transpired. Speaking of my friends,

Sophia has followed in her mother's footsteps and is now the esteemed mayor of Sunnybrook, Georgia. Liam has ventured into directing and has achieved great success, directing numerous blockbusters and earning recognition as one of the foremost film directors of our time, receiving accolades across the globe.

Additionally, Sophia and Liam have married and are now anticipating the birth of their third child. As for me, I pursued a career as an author and have published several books that present mythology in a modern context. I found love and married a wonderful man named Elijah Sanders, who also happens to be my publisher. The two of us reside in Sunnybrook, Georgia, where we are raising our daughter, Amelia. My journey as an author commenced after I *self-published a book a few years back, which delved into the various perspectives that my friends and I had about that fateful day. It was a tale of how three societal outcasts transcended their circumstances, saved the world, and evolved into new versions of themselves. To this day, I am often asked whether our account of events is true, and I always reply with the same question: If you believe it to be true, then why couldn't it be? You might be curious to know the title of the book I penned. Well, I named it **"Book of Cerberus."***

About the Author

Atticus Blackwood is a talented author hailing from Athens, GA, whose literary works seamlessly blend the genres of realistic fiction, mystery, and supernatural elements, creating a captivating and unique reading experience. His stories transport both young adult and adult readers to immersive worlds that skillfully merge the ordinary with the extraordinary, weaving together suspense and intrigue. Atticus is known for his writing style, which effortlessly combines a casual and approachable tone with expert storytelling prowess, allowing readers to deeply connect with his well-crafted characters and enthralling narratives. Fueled by a deep-seated passion for creating compelling adventures, Atticus has the remarkable ability to transform everyday moments into extraordinary tales that continue to resonate with readers long after they've finished reading.